MW00535472

Written and Illustrated by

Thomas "Tommy" Hopkins Glatthaar

A Tommy Glatthaar Production

Background

Once upon a time... Man I always wanted to say that because they always say that in fairy tales. Anyway, my name is Arthur Hopkins. My friends call me Shorty. I was born on Tuesday, June 14th, 1966, and I lived in the apartment at 14 Stuyvesant Oval 10D in New York City.

I was a boy, a little boy with brown hair, brown eyes and the amazing ability to never sit still. I did not speak clearly until I was 6 years old. I didn't always understand what people said to me.

Sometimes people thought I was being disobedient, but I honestly did not always understand. I also didn't understand social cues. Everyone in a room might be getting on their coats, but I didn't understand it was time to leave. I liked to line up all my books and if anybody bumped into my arrangements, I would scream, cry and holler. Needless to say I was not an easy child to live with. Some people thought I was abrasive, argumentative, mischievous, jealous, greedy, narcissistic, antagonistic, immature, manipulative, loud-mouth, selfish, spoiled, self-centered, arrogant, stubborn, egotistical, controlling, irritating, disruptive, bossy, closed-minded, rebellious, and headstrong. Sometimes, I feel like my behavior was criticized for being far more villainous than it really was. I don't like feeling like a bad guy. Besides, I don't like judgmental people.

I didn't allow anyone in my room then and still do not. Many people call me crazy, but I need privacy. I don't like when my fashion sense is criticized or if I get in trouble for losing things. I also hate when people are critical of other people's houses. I'm also afraid of getting in trouble and facing consequences for my actions. Trust me: I'm a coward. I like to do the coolest things like reading books and watching movies and do not like when other people try to borrow my things. I know they say sharing is caring, but I don't think it's always caring. I'm a "getter" and I'm afraid of other "getters" like myself. They sometimes accidentally lose things and I get disappointed. I keep my thoughts to myself because no one will ever understand. I want to explain to people why I do things. Sometimes I forget what to say. I don't want to leave people confused. I also don't swear. But I allow other people to swear.

Also, I don't like change, well not all changes. Because for starters, sometimes I feel like everybody is after me and I don't know what to do about it. The other thing is that whenever people ask if they can borrow something from me, I'm afraid they'll lose them or have them all to themselves. But I think the most positive thing about change is that it's like a magical life-changing adventure with my parents.

****

　　　Speaking of my parents, they have always wanted me to
have a good education. I went to speech therapy twice a week as well
as OT, for many years. At first I find it complicated, but I eventually
learned to socialize.

My mother, Betty, is a strong, confident, overprotective, strict, tough, courageous, easily irritated, caring, responsible, fun-loving, short-tempered, honest, and independent woman. She is a former social worker and studies people to make sure that everything is okay. I find that pretty creepy. Sometimes, we can have major disagreements and I call her a nag. She is often critical of my poor behavior and thoroughly disgusted with being bossed around by me. Combined with the endless chores and no help or even a simple "thank you" for all the work she does she can become very frustrated. Mom also likes to read and enjoys solving people's problems. She has a long time interest in real estate and checks out people's houses. The way she is always looking at houses made me feel like my parents wanted to move.

My father Russell was an intelligent hard worker, who watched the news to find out what's going on in the world. He also watched sitcoms almost every night. I may have major disagreements with my parents, but they taught me important life lessons that go on in this world. Dad also loved telling stories about history because he believed that history is a powerful force that affects people's lives every day. People are not even conscious of it.

I've got to tell you, parents tend to be fairly temperamental and sarcastic with everyone. While this was usually reasonable, considering how my sister Molly or I tended to disobey rules and get into trouble, at times their temper got the better of them and they jumped to conclusions. This caused them not to listen to the whole story. Seriously, every time I try talking to Mom about different situations, she covers her ears to protect herself because she doesn't want to hear excuses. She calls me insane. Sometimes, Mom gets so aggravated like she isn't sure if I had autism and she thinks I should act normal. Like what Mom always said, "Actions are more important than words."

To Mom, someone who doesn't appreciate her concerns is attacking her. For example, she thinks I should keep my room cleaner, and if I don't listen to her she gets really mad. Dad always protects Mom and always takes Mom's side during arguments with either Molly or me. Dad can sometimes be scarier than Mom. Sometimes, I honestly believed whenever people get into heated arguments, it's like they get psychologically consumed by their own evil dark side and transforms them into raging monsters, turning everyone against each other. It's scary.

Whenever something bothers them, they complain to each other about it. Sometimes I wish I could do something about it. I don't want to be completely hard on them because revenge is for bad guys and I'm not a bad guy. I learned from a cartoon that even when people are upset with you, they still love you. The special thing is you could never lose their love no matter what. Pretty touching, isn't it?

When Mom and Dad were really stressed and angry, Mom tended to uncharacteristically snap at Molly or me. Later she would regret deep down for being so angry. Of course, this happened when neither of us was in sight.

Nonetheless, they are protective of their family, particularly me, and will attack anyone and defend us from any threat. They loved Molly and me more than anyone or anything in the world and did all they can to keep us from harm. They are kind and hardworking, and they proved that while they are somewhat irritable, they can also be compassionate and understanding as they usually forgive Molly and me for our antics. You know what they say; everyone has hardships and problems in their lives, no matter what age.

They met in Providence during their freshman year in college. They were good friends for years and then they decided to be a couple. Eventually, they got married and had children. My big sister Molly and I were both born at Jacobi Hospital in the Bronx. Every time my father came home from work, he always warned me: "Work is not play."

All my life I was interested in cartoons and movies, including previews and commercials. When I got introduced to VHS and tried it out, I was thrilled. I tried to speak clearly, but I had so many thoughts about every movie in my head. I liked it. My parents were concerned because they didn't think I was focusing on reality. They gave me pills to control my OCD behavior, much to my dismay because of the pill's taste. I was growing up, learning a lot of things from cartoons I watched and from my family and friends who cared about me. I'm utterly and eternally grateful. I don't like being forced to do anything for people, but I don't like disappointing people even more. I like to help and be there for people no matter what. I owe them all everything. I even got a job at my favorite video store, Blockbuster, because I loved movies. I also have a strong interest in doing jigsaw puzzles and putting them in frames. My mother says that it is good for your brain.

****

As soon as I graduated high school, I lost some people I loved. A good friend of mine died in a tragic car accident and my father died from prostate cancer and diabetes. I miss them so much.

My mother taught me that heaven is a home and we're only on this Earth for a while. We are in heaven for all eternity. Just like Molly and me, Mom loves and misses her husband very much and is usually depressed on the anniversary of the day he died.

I wish that everything is like a cartoon and I could have an adventure like defeating bad guys and saving lives. I don't want to be a police officer, a firefighter, a doctor, or a scientist. I want to be the kind of hero shown in movies and cartoons. I could be a knight saving a princess locked in a tower or a superhero rescuing a damsel in distress.

This reminds me, I want romance because there's so much of it in the world. I wish I could have it too. I've tried to hit on girls like my former babysitter, girls at school, and one of my sister's friends. Unfortunately, they all didn't work out. One night, my father explained how to win girls: be patient.

Speaking of my sister, after Molly graduated from Syracuse University, she left the apartment to travel around the world.

I always believed that the real world is boring. Like I said before, I always think everything should be like a cartoon. Unfortunately people in the real world don't survive the stunts like cartoon characters do.

Despite the fact I don't focus on reality, my parents explained to me about the Moon Landing with Neil Armstrong, the Vietnam War, the John Lennon murder, the Reagan attempted assassination, the Space Shuttle Challenger disaster and everything else that happened in this world. I complained to them, "Why is there so much evil in the world?" Even they don't know. Since then, I became really interested in historical events, no matter what it is. Good or bad.

There are many people in this world who think that people should be cured of autism. I don't think so. My mind is constantly running in my head and I talk to myself in order to act out the voices from cartoons and movies. Mom warned me that people don't always understand that and explained that people with a mental disorder called schizophrenia talk to the voices in their heads as though the voices are real people. People with autism apparently talk to themselves in order to act out... Oh wait I already said that. Sorry. Sometimes when I talk to myself, I feel like there's cartoon characters in my head. I think they apparently help me socialize.

There is one thing I know about this. I'm proud of having autism because I am proud of who I am, how God made me, and I accept differences. Besides, my whole life is like a piece of a puzzle.

****

Oh, I almost forgot to tell you guys. There's a female lead in this story. Her name is Samantha Johnson. Her friends call her Sammy. Unlike me, she doesn't have autism. Sammy was born in Westerly, Rhode Island on Wednesday, May 20, 1970. and lived in the apartment at 29 Cooper Street 3D in New York City.

When Sammy was a little girl, her life was good and happy. Her mother, Ann Patricia sang her own song called "Love Wins" until Sammy fell asleep. Her father, Anthony, worked as a salesman at a car dealership. She is an avid sports player. Sammy enjoys swimming, bowling, hockey, tennis, and other sports. Sammy also loves literature and unlike me, she is quite organized. Sammy has a big moral compass. She is a gifted singer and a great dancer, although she hides it. Sammy is always overbooked with her schedules. Sammy is also pure of heart, intelligent, compassionate, caring, sympathetic, outspoken, headstrong, and a loyal friend. Sammy always performs acts of self-sacrifice and courage. She is very mature, responsible, lovely, fierce, fun and a true feminist. Her parents taught her how to be a remarkable person and she appreciates everyone around her for who she or he is. They even taught her to be generous and it's only right to share our blessing and offer help through life's different journeys. Sammy wanted to be there for others. It's good to be an ambassador of compassion. Pretty nice, huh? This inspired her to help the poor by giving them food. Sammy is willing to forgive people for their wrongdoings, unless they can't be reasoned with.

Sammy was very well-liked by most of the teachers throughout her life. She pays attention to what the professors have to say and she tries real hard to do her best in all her classes. Sammy becomes the other students' peer mentor. Despite that, there was a barrier between her and other children her age when she was a child. Sammy's high intellect and liberal political views did not always make her popular. Therefore, she is a bit of a loner and social outcast. She has some friends by her side like her best friends, Maureen Myllek and Caitlin Oliver.

When she was 13 years old, her mother gave birth to a boy and named him, Mikey. When Sammy held Mikey in her arms for the first time, she vowed to be a good sister to Mikey and protect him no matter what. His first word was actually, "Sammy." Pretty cute, huh?

Sadly, their parents died in a plane crash. Sammy and Mikey were sent to live with their grandparents in New York City. Sammy has been trying to deal with her loss ever since. If you guys are wondering where her grandfather is, he died during the Vietnam War. When Joan reported to Sammy about her parents, she refused to believe it at first. This tragedy emotionally traumatized Sammy and she refused to talk about it, not even with Mikey, Joan, Maureen, Caitlin, or Jerome. The sad part is that when the reality hits that your deceased loved ones won't share any of your special moments, an overwhelming sadness really takes hold. Despite that, she still remained a wonderful and friendly person.

Joan has always been a loving, overprotective, stern, temperamental, tough, strict, a bit overbearing, caring, and well-meaning lady. She raised them after their parents died. It was difficult for Sammy ever since. Joan gets concerned about Sammy's despair. But that's not the only problem Sammy has in her life.

****

When she reached high school, Sammy got attracted to a handsome guy named Jack "Shark" Roderick Jr. She thought Shark was the cutest boy ever. She didn't know he was so dangerous at the time and also 12 years older than she was.

Shark hid it very well and always hung out where the high school kids were, like the roller-skating rink and the hamburger place. Sammy felt "invisible" except around her best friend Maureen, Maureen's partner Caitlin, her annoying and shy little brother Mikey, and her overprotective grandmother Joan. Sammy thought if she dated Shark, she wouldn't be "invisible" anymore. She didn't realize that Shark only cared about her appearance. Shark seemed nice enough when they first started interacting with one another. However, things took a turn for the worse.

Shark is the main villain of this story. He is a good looking, Caucasian male, 6'3", with a short black hair-cut, brown eyes, and fair skin. He is smooth as silk, and silver-tongued. He wears a black leather jacket, white tank top undershirts, and black boots. He always wears a gold cross necklace. Shark is fanatically religious. He has a serious mental problem that made him devote his life to being a "Christian." Shark believes he is fixing all of "God's mistakes" and he is very creepy. Shark always quotes scary Bible passages because he thinks it's how the world should work. He is in excellent physical shape from years of combat training. He is also really smart. He can speak at least five languages, including English, French, Russian, Italian, and Spanish.

Shark is an outright lying, hot-tempered, rebellious troublemaker. He is an immense jerk and lacks any compassion. Shark feels no guilt over terrorizing anyone who gets in his way. He is very clever, threatening, and takes immense pleasure in other people's misfortunes. He is very charismatic and can be very cordial. That's what makes him so despicable and dangerous. Nothing justifies his crimes. Shark cannot feel empathy for others and never tries to redeem himself. Shark enjoys tormenting his victims. He is uncomfortable with people who have disabilities because he considers disabled people as "God's mistakes," especially people with autism. He is filled with hate and disgust for them and is hell-bent on killing them. Shark is perfectly fine if anyone is discriminated against for any reason. This would include age, class, color, disability, gender, height, language, looks, mental condition, race/ethnicity/nationality, rank, other people's religion, sex, size and species. He uses disability-related terms with negative connotations like *"cripple," "daft," "dim-witted," "feeble-minded," "idiotic," "madman," and "retarded."*

He is pure evil at heart, and more than willing to get rid of anyone, even children who are disabled or anyone else who stands in his way. Shark is what many would consider a classic villain. He is extremely dark, greedy, violent and sadistic.

He has an extremely high opinion of himself. Shark considers himself "God's perfect child."

Shark has a negative philosophy about anyone being different. He believes that they're nothing special and only made to be "God's ultimate disgrace." Shark always felt revulsion and anger towards them, which means a sense of disgust and loathing. He stated that all of "God's mistakes" were made to be crucified and burned in hell for their "sins." The most frightening quality is that he covers up his evil nature very effectively. He finds the notion of love to be a complete illusion. Shark never showed any kindness toward anyone around him, not Sammy nor the Hamilton Brothers (more about them later). He was something of a hater of all mankind, and took to callously bullying both his henchmen and his targets alike.

Since Shark was ignored as a child, he never developed a sense of morality, of knowing the difference between right and wrong. Shark believes himself to be a magnanimous person, claiming that he is the "Spirit of All That Is Right," while at the same time accusing everyone else of being the "Axis of Evil." He commits acts that are atrocious, yet he never recognizes that he has done anything wrong.

Shark is also very hostile and he has a strong aversion toward people. He is intolerant of failure, berating the Hamilton Brothers for their mistakes and problems. Shark was also very charismatic and persuasive... Oh wait I've already said that, Sorry. When they started dating, Shark turned out to be a big mistake. He psychologically and physically abused Sammy badly. I'll explain the rest of the situation later in the story.

One night when Shark explained his backstory to Sammy, she immediately made an excuse to leave. When she got home, she called and broke up with him. Near the end of the call, Shark threatened her.

Sammy complained to her grandmother about it because she couldn't take it anymore. She and her grandmother reported Shark's crimes to the police. Sammy was aware that you have to explain these situations to the police. The police suspected that Shark was involved in hurting the dog and beating up Gary, but could not get enough evidence to bring charges against him. Shark considered them "Pigs" or "Snakes." Shark became over-obsessed with getting Sammy back and has been stalking her ever since. When will he ever leave her alone?

****

When she graduated from high school, Sammy got a scholarship to Fordham University, which made Joan so proud. She eventually got a job at CVS to work her way through college. Sammy is a senior college student at Fordham University. Sammy is always overbooked with her schedules.

Ever since her parents died, Sammy acts more like a mother figure to Mikey than Joan. Sammy is determined to teach Mikey how to be a polite and respectful child. She had him doing community service as they wore reflective vests and picked up trash along the interstate with poles and bags. Of course, Mikey complains about it. Although she finds him annoying because of his constant teasing, they care about each other like all brothers and sisters should. Mikey is also apparently shy, critical, good-hearted, impatient, mischievous, blunt, well-intentioned, brave, friendly, loyal, fun-loving, and playful. Whenever he gets in trouble, Sammy scolds him and makes him repeat the lessons that Joan had impressed upon him.

Sammy always wanted to be a therapist to solve people's problems. Unlike Shark, Sammy likes helping kids with disabilities, new kids at school, and kids who were being picked on.

In order to find someone who can hang out with me, Mom decided to hire a "community habilitation" (comm. hab.) worker. When Mom found the resume about Sammy and her school record, Mom and I thought she should call Sammy to see if she would be available in case I want to do some things on my own.

****

Plot

In the present day, it was late 1991, I was planning to relax and watch some cartoons, but unfortunately, my mother set up a meeting today. After my best friend Butchie left for work, Mom started knocking on my door.

"SHORTY!!! Hurry up! We're going to be late for your meeting!"

My mother yelled from behind the door. I didn't respond. Mom always thinks I'm trying to ignore her whenever she calls for me. She doesn't always understand my autism and feels unappreciated. When I don't answer her she feels like dirt. Mom has no choice but to use her secret dangerous weapon to get my attention: her screeching tone.

She yelled again, "SHOOORTY!!!"

Meanwhile, I was distracted watching the end of a show in my room and I didn't want to miss how the episode ended. Like my high school teacher Mrs. Anderson said at the last meeting, I don't stop until something is done. I think she's right. While I was listening to the music on TV, I was also dancing and pretending I was in a musical on stage, imagining myself in a fancy 40s top hat, suit, and cane.

After she hollered my name again, my mother opened the door, and ended my fantasy. Seriously, every time my Mom barges into my room, I feel like my Mom is trying to undermine every single fantasy I'm having.

I thought to myself, "Uh oh, nag-alert!"

She yelled, "Shorty, we have a meeting today and you're laying around. We have to get you a shirt with a collar on it, some long pants and you have to take your pill."

Annoyed, I yelled "ALL RIGHT, MOM! I'LL GET READY AND TAKE THE PILL! You also don't have to open the door without knocking."

"Look, Shorty," Mom replied. "I can come in if I want to. Besides we have a meeting today, so get ready."

I didn't even know we had a meeting today. Mom always thought that people with autism couldn't make their own decisions without their parents' supervision like a child.

My mother and I were getting some fancy clothes for the meeting. Mom complained since my room is messy, "Seriously, how can anyone live in this garbage heap?"

I responded as she sighed, "What are you talking about, Mom? Every item here has its own purpose."

She says that she won't live in a pig pen. If she has to speak to me about this again, she might have to call the cops on me and kick me out. After she gave the clothes to me, she left. I put the clothes on and went into the kitchen. She thought I looked good.

Before I left, I checked to make sure my bedroom door was closed. Mom calls it OCD (Obsessive Compulsive Disorder). I just don't want my sister's dog, Cinnamon to enter my room. She is asleep on the couch. I explained earlier that I do not like to be told what to do and I don't like when people go into my room.

Since I live in my mother's apartment, she thinks she can make all the rules. So what if I keep things instead of throwing them away. She doesn't see it that way! If she just left me alone, I wouldn't have to yell.

Mom stated, "Shorty, You're going to have to grow up one day. You'll never be happy if you waste all your time goofing off."

I responded as my Mom sighed, "Oh yeah? Just watch me."

Mom always has been aggravated by my ridiculousness and she feels like she wants to throw me out. "*Dammit* Shorty, you're making me crazy." Mom said quietly.

Warning! Swearing Alert!

The words in bold and italic are bad words in the story. Kids, in case you don't know what it means, ask your parents.

Parents, if you don't want your kids to say these words, explain what it means and that way they'll understand.

****

Meanwhile, Sammy was sleeping until her alarm clock beeped at 5:30 in the morning. It's like Mom's thing. She always gets up with the sun. Sammy finds that having to get up so early in the morning is a little annoying. Her hair looks really shaggy when she wakes up.

She started her day by jogging and studying French on a tape recorder like she usually does. Sammy was wearing spandex exercise clothes and her hair was in a ponytail. She feels better when she exercises.

After jogging, Sammy went home to take a shower, and get ready for a meeting with me today. When she was about to leave, her grandmother Joan asked Sammy to walk Mikey to school, because she has a big schedule today.

"Morning, Dear." Joan said. "I need a favor."

"Sure, Nana." Sammy replied.

"I need you to make breakfast for Mikey and walk him to school today." Joan explained. "I have to go to the store to get some ingredients for tonight's dinner."

"Okay, Nana." Sammy replied. "but I have a very important meeting today and I have to go to work afterwards."

"Fine by me, honey." Joan said, "as long as nothing happens to you."

"Nana!" Sammy sighed. She's always annoyed with her grandmother's overprotectiveness with herself and Mikey, although she understands why she does it.

"Sorry, Dear." Joan said. "I mean after what's happening with you, I just don't want you to get hurt."

"Don't worry, Nana." Sammy explained. "I'll be alright."

"You're wonderful, Dear." Joan replied as she kissed her on the cheek and walked out the door. "I'm off."

After Joan left, Sammy woke up Mikey. He complained that he doesn't want to go to school, much to Sammy's annoyance. "You're going whether you like it or not!"

Later after Sammy got Mikey prepared for school, they exited the building. What they don't know is that there is a mysterious figure hiding in the bushes in an alleyway nearby. It happens to be Shark. He has been spying on Sammy since she broke up with him and Shark vows to do whatever it takes to win her back. However, he needs two idiots to spy on Sammy for him.

****

The Hamilton Brothers are both the comic reliefs in this story. Victor Hamilton is a good person, but he has done some very bad things. He has brown-colored eyes, slightly tan skin, and short dark brown hair with bangs, which are often mistaken or made fun of as "emo hair" or an "emo flap". However, some people actually like his haircut. Victor is often shown as smarter, more obedient, and more mature than Billy Hamilton (though their personalities are hardly different), as he often knows much more about the world than Billy does.

Victor is tall and slim with brown curly hair. He is the better-looking of the two brothers, and he often teases his brother about that fact. He is also smarter than his brother and is constantly playing tricks and pranks on him, but has little patience for his less-intelligent brother. That said, he is far from a rocket scientist: in fact, he is self-conscious about his lack of intelligence. That made him and his brother easy prey for someone like Shark: a strong, smart and assertive character who knows what he wants and is not afraid to use his skills to get it. Shark has the Hamilton Brothers completely intimidated.

Billy Hamilton is shorter and skinnier than his brother. He has brown hair and a beard. For as long as he can remember his brother has been beating him up and taking his stuff, and he has always resented it. He also has a strange compunction to get his brother to like and accept him.

Those guys also still lived with their parents, who are too busy condemning each other to realize their boys were working for Shark. I understand what they go through with that. Seriously, they're like a couple of cartoon characters or the Three Stooges whenever they get involved. There are always lots of accidents! Sad thing about them is that ever since they moved to New York City years ago, they have never fit in and always been treated like losers. This is how the boys meet Shark.

The boys were beaten up and humiliated by a group of kids. They decided to take the shortcut home.

"God," Victor complained. "These brats are a major pain in the **ass**!"

"Ugh!" Billy replied. "Tell me about it, Vic!"

"You know what?" Victor said. "Sometimes I wish there is someone in our lives who would watch our backs."

"Yeah!" Billy shouted.

"Well your wish is granted." the intensive voice said. The boys are startled and confused by the voice. They keep turning their heads to find out who it is.

"Who said that?" Victor asked.

"Yeah." Billy said. "Are you a ghost?"

"I did," the voice said as the Hamilton Brothers turned towards the alleyway. The figure walked out of the shadows and is revealed to be Shark. He explained who he was. Shark acted like he was lonely and he wanted some friends. They did not realize he wanted to surround himself with weak people that he could control. Finally, the Hamilton Brothers felt accepted. "Are you interested in having some fun?"

"Sure." Victor said.

"I'm in." Billy said.

"Good," Shark said with a grin. "because I have a little proposition for both of you."

****

While Mom and I were walking to the meeting, I was explaining to her about this cartoon I saw before she barged in. As I was quoting the scene, she didn't know how to quote as much as I do. Mom explained, "Shorty, I can't remember the quotes from the cartoons as much as you do." I always rewind the videos because I always enjoyed the scenes and the quotes. Apparently, it makes me think clearly.

When we got to the meeting at the New York Training Resources, we greeted everyone, like one of my old teachers. There was a beautiful girl at the meeting. Her name was Samantha Johnson. She told us that her friends call her Sammy.

They said she is training to be a therapist and she is doing that by being my new community habilitation worker. With her help, I will be able to go places without my mother. Thank God.

"Hi, I'm Sammy and you must be Shorty." I was speaking gibberish as a response, which made Sammy giggle.

Embarrassed, Mom stopped me from gibbering more, "Shorty! Stop that!!"

It was distracting to have such a pretty girl at my meeting, but we had to discuss my future.

One day, I would like to have an apartment of my own near my job at my favorite video store, Blockbuster.

Sammy asked me "What Blockbuster do you work at?"

I responded. "I work at the one right next to the drug store, CVS."

"No kidding," Sammy responded. "I work at the drug store next door."

I asked "Really?!"

Sammy responded, "Yeah."

Sammy explained that she is working there while she is in college at Fordham University. She asked me how I like working at Blockbuster.

"I work there because I love movies," I explained. "I always stock videos on different shelves in alphabetical order, because you know they have different categories: Action, Adventure, Comedy, Drama, Family-Favorite, Fantasy, Horror, Romance, Science Fiction, Thriller and many more. It kinda smells funny, well not in a bad way, but I still like to go there. It's like you're in a video city there. You can also get some food there like you're going to the movies."

As I continued talking, Mom used her hand like a puppet to show Sammy that I talk too much. Sammy nodded. Sometimes, my mother doesn't understand the words I'm saying. She even warned Sammy that her ears will bleed if I talk too much. I know that's not true.

While we were chatting, I thought to myself that Sammy is like many of the movie characters I have seen. She seems to be pure of heart, unconventional, empathetic, intelligent, compassionate, graceful, selfless, educated, sophisticated, caring, sympathetic, sweet, bibliophilic, assertive, outspoken, curious, feisty, kind-hearted, loyal, noble, gentle, sensible, spirited, understanding, heroic, motherly, sensitive, pleasant, incorruptible, forgiving, and a friend. She is very mature, responsible, lovely, and fun. I'm a good judge of character.

We discussed where I would live in the future, after I move out of my mother's apartment. Sammy said, "You're a friendly guy Shorty. I'm sure you can find a nice roommate." The other people at the meeting agreed with Sammy and they would help me find a roommate.

I replied as I blushed, "Oh, um...thank you."

Mom reminded me as she whispered, "Shorty, this is an interview, not a date."

I replied, "Come on, Mom, we're just having a nice conversation."

We also talked about how much I would like to be able to drive a car. I also need to learn how to keep my apartment clean.

Mom complained at the meeting how messy my room at home is and I told everyone, "See what I mean. I need to get out of her apartment and do things my way." Mom rolled her eyes in exasperation.

Finally, I also explained that I liked to do music with my favorite guitar. Mom explained that I'm a guitarist and I'm having trouble trying to come up with my own song. Sammy thought that maybe she can help me with that since she is into music herself.

Later, after the meeting was over, Mom asked, "So Sammy, when will you be free to hang out with Shorty?"

Sammy explained that she has a really busy schedule. She looked in her own schedule book. "Tuesdays are usually good for me. How about I call you later and we can decide what would be a good day?" I was jealous that Mom and Sammy gave each other their phone numbers. "Hey, no fair!" I shouted. "Why can't I have her phone number?"

"We'll talk soon." Sammy replied. "Okay, Shorty?"

"Okay, bye, Sammy!" I said breathlessly.

As we were leaving the building, I was daydreaming about the movie based fantasy I want to have with Sammy. I could be Superman and she could be Lois Lane or I could be Spider-Man and she could be Mary Jane Watson. See what I mean about living in a fantasy world?

****

After the meeting, Sammy headed toward CVS, the one that is next door to Blockbuster where I work. Sammy's boss, Jerome Myllek, is very respectful. He has always been like a father figure to Sammy and is deeply concerned about tough situations in her life, like her parents' tragic deaths and her bad relationship with her evil ex-boyfriend. Jerome was also Sammy's father's best friend and he is trying to be there for her.

Sammy said, "Hey, Boss."

Jerome responded, "Samantha! How's my girl?"

Sammy stated, "Good, so what time do I have to come here over the weekend?"

Jerome explained, "10-4 Saturday and 9-5 Sunday."

Sammy was glad she is working for Jerome at the drug-store. Like she said at the meeting, she only plans on working at the drug store while she's a student at Fordham.

Jerome's daughter, who is Sammy's best friend, Maureen Myllek, asked Sammy, "Hey, girl. What's going on?"

Sammy told Maureen about this morning's meeting and her new client Shorty; that's me.

As soon as Sammy finished her story, Maureen's partner, Caitlin Oliver, showed up to get her prescription. The girls and Jerome greeted Caitlin, as they were happy to see her.

"Hey, girls." Caitlin said. "What's the good word?"

Sammy wanted to explain to Caitlin about her new client, but Maureen complained, "Oh no, I can't listen to that again!"

Maureen always protected Sammy from bullies. She has always had a rebellious streak, expressed in her punk-style clothing. She is suspended from high school temporarily because she shoved a classmate who was bullying Sammy down the locker hallway and beat her up with her karate skills. The girl was yelling insults at Sammy, calling her a "loser", and when Maureen approached the scene she became extremely angry. Shoving someone was not the brightest idea, but at the time, Maureen's temper got the best of her. She goes to a counselor to deal with anger issues. Maureen also studied martial arts.

****

Meanwhile at the nearby jewelry store, two security guards were walking down the hallway, chatting with each other. They didn't realize that some thieves somehow snuck into the door.

One guard asked, "So what are we guarding this necklace for???"

The other guard shouts, "We're getting paid to watch it, not stand around yapping. Shut up and do your job."

The guard replied, "Ok..."

They waited quietly for a few seconds until the guard asked, "So...did ya see that new action hero movie that just came out?"

The other guard shouts, "What did I JUST say?"

The guard replied, "Something about lunch?"

The other guard asked, "Are you stupid?"

The guard explained, "My mom said I was dropped on my head as a baby; is that it?"

The other guard asked, "Do you even work here...?"

The guard replied, "Depends what work is!!!!"

The other guard sounded frustrated, "I've got nothing else to say to you. You're ridiculous." He turned away from him.

Suddenly, the guard mysteriously disappeared. Someone grabbed his shirt from behind and covered his mouth so he couldn't scream. He was pulled out of the way. The other guard was relieved and said to himself, "I'm glad he left, I get sick of hearing that guy's voice." All of a sudden he was knocked out by one of the crooks behind him.

Neither guard noticed that three mysterious figures in the shadows were sneaking into a different room...Oh yeah, I've already said that, sorry. They were wearing black masks and black outfits. They spotted a beautiful diamond necklace. The large tough looking one stopped the others because he was aware of the invisible lasers that were revealed. The tough one had great reflexes, much to their surprise. He easily removed the glass and retrieved the necklace. This set off the alarm, but the thieves successfully escaped. As soon as they left, the guards realized that the diamond necklace was gone. The crooks pulled off their masks and the leader said to a picture in his hand, "It's all for you, Samantha."

****

Later that night I was at my favorite sports bar, the
Teammates, with my Mom, one of my best friends, Butchie
Camastro, his girlfriend Stephanie Beck, and Stephanie's mother,
Diane, who is also Mom's good friend. Diane is such a good friend
and they talk so much that sometimes I think she is my mother's
therapist. They're always telling each other their concerns about their
children.

I've known Butchie since we were kids. We became best
buddies after I helped him cross the monkey bars on the playground
by grabbing his legs. I also find him pretty funny. He is tall, slim
with blond hair and blue eyes. Butchie always agrees with people
and loves cars, soda, and burping. His parents got divorced when he
was little. His father, Butchie Sr. moved to California and Butchie
was living with his mother in New York. When Butchie got a little
older, his mother Karen got remarried and decided to move, but
Butchie didn't want to leave and I did not want to be separated from

him. His mother decided to let Butchie stay at our place and my mother agreed.

As for Stephanie, his girlfriend, she is always full of fun and excitement. She is a little shorter than Butchie and me and has brown hair and brown eyes. When Butchie and I reached middle school, we met Stephanie in the classroom. She had a huge crush on Butchie. They were starting to hang out with each other. At first, I was jealous because I felt ignored. Eventually, I realized that Stephanie and I also have many things in common. She became my second best friend. Butchie eventually got a job at the Fordham cafeteria: cleaning the tables, pushing the chairs into the tables, and taking out the trash. Stephanie got a job at an agency for people with developmental disabilities: helping people with basketball, bowling, and going to the movies. She calls her own mother by her first name. Although Stephanie doesn't like movies too much, she still likes to spend time with her friends.

Butchie and Stephanie were both smiling and holding hands while they sat down across the table.

Stephanie asked, "Isn't this lovely, Butchie?"

Butchie replied, "Very lovely, Babe?"

Stephanie explained. "I like being here; they have good food."

Butchie agreed, "They do."

Stephanie continued, "I hope they bring our drinks."

Butchie responded, "Yeah, I hope they bring our drinks. I can't wait for them."

Stephanie was excited, "I hope they don't take too long. We have tickets. We have to go see this movie that's coming next week. Oh my God." I don't get why she just changed the subject like that. It makes no sense.

Butchie responded, "Yeah. That's going to be a blast."

Stephanie replied, "Yes I know."

Butchie said, "It's gonna be huge."

Stephanie agreed, "Yes. Huge. Huge. Huge. Huge excitement."

Butchie continued to agree with her, "Yep."

Stephanie said, "It's going to be so lovely. Let's see. Not, not literally though."

Butchie replied, "Yeah, yeah. Not literally."

I get a little jealous because I really wish I could have a girlfriend who loves me.

During our high school days, I remember Butchie and I got into big fights because he was spending time with Stephanie more than me. I still feel bad about it. Besides, if they're happy, I'm happy. None of those things matter; what matters is that we're best friends no matter what happens.

When the waitress arrived with our drinks, Stephanie said, "Oooo, look at the drinks. Here they are."

Butchie replied, "Yeah, right?"

As I thanked her, the waitress asked, "What's my name, Shorty?"

While I tried to guess, the waitress pretended to be upset. Mom whispered, "Daphne."

I asked quietly, "What?"

Mom whispered in my ear, "Daphne."

When I thanked Daphne, she smiled and gave me a high five as she replied, "You are so correct, sir."

Daphne asked, "Have you all decided? But I know what you're going to have, Shorty." I laughed in response.

After Daphne finished taking our orders, she left. As I was drinking water and apple juice with no ice and no lemons, just straws, Butchie and Stephanie finished their drinks quickly.

Stephanie said as she and Butchie put the cups down, "That was so good."

Butchie replied, "Ah, that's good."

Stephanie said, "Oh my God, Butchie, I love being with you."

Butchie replied, "I love being with you too, Babe."

Stephanie said, "I know. This is so funny."

Sometimes it's as though those two speak a secret language!

Everyone else at the restaurant was talking about the important college basketball game. All I was thinking about was my romantic fantasy with Sammy.

The owners of the bar, Ace McLoughlin and his wife Gloria McLoughlin showed up to greet everyone at my table. They're always good people to me, my Mom, Molly, Butchie, Stephanie and everyone they know. We are also their favorite customers. Ace is a former athlete.

Ace greeted us as he gave me a big squeeze hug, "Hey, Shorty. How's my guy?"

I replied, "Hey, Ace."

Gloria said as she gave me a big squeeze hug. "SHORTY!!!! HOW ARE YOU?!"

I replied. "Hey, Gloria."

I turned to Ace and asked him, "Um, Ace. I got a question."

Ace replied, "What's that, son?"

I explained, "Well, there is this girl I saw today and I want to know how to impress her."

Ace and Gloria said together smoothly as they were looking at each other, "Oooo!!!!"

Mom shook her head as she already explained that Sammy is not my girlfriend.

"Well, Shorty." Ace explained to me, "If you want to win a girl's heart, always try to look your best, be clean shaven and dress nicely."

Mom reminded me that Sammy is not my girlfriend. I responded that I'm not in love with Sammy. I just think she's a very nice girl. Besides, I just met her. I didn't know much about Sammy yet. Mom gave me some quarters for the arcade in the corner of the Teammates. It's like part bar and part arcade.

"Alright, Mom. Come on, guys." I said as Stephanie, Butchie and I went to the arcade side of the bar.

Butchie, Stephanie and I made up our own storyline for the characters of the game. I played the hero of the game, Butchie and Stephanie played the villains of the game.

While Butchie, Stephanie and I were playing, my Mom was telling Ace, Gloria and Diane about my new staff person Sammy. Mom explained, "She's going to help Shorty learn new things and go to different places without having me around."

"Oh that's great, Betty." Diane said, "But what will you be doing while he's not around?"

"Maybe I'll clean his room while he's out because I am always afraid of his temper tantrums when I go into his room." Mom explained, "It would be easier to clean when he's not around."

Suddenly, the bar's band showed up to play music. The three female singers called "The Westerly Gals" are really entertaining and good singers together. Apparently, they named themselves after their hometown, Westerly, Rhode Island. Mom says it's a very nice place.

It's like a Broadway musical with these girls. The leader of the Westerly Gals is named Maria and the others named Katie and Michele. Maria always has big brainstorms for lyrics and wants to make her band as perfect as possible. The music was loud, but my friends and I liked it. My mother, Diane and her bandmates secretly didn't like Maria because of her smug and self-absorbed attitude. I would have rather finished the game than watch the show.

"Hey, Babe." Butchie asked Stephanie, "Do you want to dance?"

"Oh, Butchie!" Stephanie responded romantically, "You have such a way with words."

Suddenly, the lights were lowered and a spotlight was on them. I finished playing a game and as they danced beautifully together like a waltz, I felt sad because I felt like I wanted to have a girlfriend too.

When the music was over, everyone applauded. They embraced and kissed passionately as someone shouted, "Go, Butchie."

Diane was smiling proudly, as she is happy to see her daughter so happy, and with a charming, good looking, and handsome young man like Butchie. The way I saw them kiss like that, I compare them to those love stories like they showed in fairy tales. I feel like I wanted to kiss a girl like Sammy, but I don't want to do it in a bad way because my father told me not to force a girl to make out with you. Besides, I always believed that time is better than force. The lights went back on. Mom thinks the bar is not the right place for smooching. She's not a PDA (public display of affection) fan! But Butchie and Stephanie are.

When Butchie and Stephanie saw me depressed, Butchie asked, "What's wrong, buddy?"

"I don't know." I responded sadly, "It's just I feel left out when I see you guys being so happy together. Sometimes I wish that I had a girlfriend too."

"Don't worry, Shorty." Stephanie stated, "I'm sure there's a girl for you. Besides, no matter what happens, you get by with a little help from your friends."

That reminds me. I forgot to tell you that we have been big fans of the Beatles all our lives. We have always enjoyed their songs and liked to quote their songs all the time. My mother was calling out for us that our dinner was there.

"Dinner's ready, guys!" Mom shouted, "You don't want the food to get cold."

We got back to our table. I got the usual: chicken fingers and French fries with some pickles and chili for dipping the fries.

Mom and Diane congratulated Butchie and Stephanie on their romantic dance. They danced very well together. Mom and I didn't want to ruin the moment for Butchie and Stephanie, so we both agreed to keep our mouths shut. Sometimes we think that Butchie and Stephanie need to learn how to get a room.

While everyone else was talking, I was thinking about movie images in my head. Sometimes it's easier to think about different shows than carrying on a conversation.

Author's note: I know it's inappropriate to make out in public. Mom and one of my teachers, Mrs. Wood taught me about this thing called PDAs. It's also known as Public Display of Affection. I thought it would be interesting to make Shorty and Betty talk about the dangers of PDAs behind Butchie and Stephanie's backs. Remember, Kids. Not everyone is comfortable about these things. Stay safe, Kids.

****

While I was at the Teammates, Sammy was working at CVS. The store was about to close for the night.

"Oh my God!" Caitlin yelled, "I left the groceries in the car! I better get them home before they go bad."

The girls kissed each other on the cheek and everyone went home. Sammy was heading back to her apartment at 29 Cooper Street 3D.

Her ex-boyfriend, Jack Roderick also known as Shark, and his two dimwitted sidekicks, Victor and Billy Hamilton, were waiting for her in front of her apartment door.

"Boo. Guess who?" Sammy was frightened to see that Shark was waiting for her.

Shark planned on winning Sammy back by giving her a diamond necklace that he and his cronies stole from a jewelry store.

He said, deviously, "Samantha, I always said I would give you the world. This is just a down payment."

Sammy coldly rejected him and handed the necklace back. "I dumped you before because you mistreated me badly, you bullied disabled people and also you cheated on me." Sammy shouted, "SO LEAVE ME ALONE!"

She stormed into her apartment, and Shark was in the hallway angry and upset. Victor and Billy were both whispering to each other about Shark's behavior.

"Do you think Shark will ever win her back, Vic?" Billy asked quietly,

"Who knows?" Victor whispered, "Maybe if he hadn't busted an artery, things would have been different right about now."

"Heh! Heh! Heh!" Billy laughed, "I don't know what that means, but good one, man."

When they giggled, Shark grabbed them by their necks, and shoved them against the wall. They always felt like weak little kids every time Shark abused them.

"You two fools are completely stupid!!" Shark told them harshly, "Now if any of you want to hang out with me, you need to shape up!! UNDERSTAND?!"

"Yes sir," The Hamiltons cried together.

"Good boys." Shark said softly as he shoved them aside to the ground.

Shark appeared to distance himself from the Hamilton Brothers by constantly shaming them. He did not care much about them and seemed to view them as tools and weapons to use for his own benefit. Shark berated and abused them. They are deeply frightened of him. Seriously, what a jerk that Shark is, huh?

Shark vowed to win Sammy back if it's the last thing he does. He will do anything to make Sammy's life a living hell now that she rejected and embarrassed him in front of Victor and Billy.

As soon as Shark angrily stormed off, Billy whispered to Victor, "Sheesh what's wrong with that guy?"

Victor scratched his chin and said, "Maybe that leather jacket is too tight on him." They tagged along after Shark.

****

The next day, Butchie and I went to the Uptown Comics store to get this week's new comics. We saw Stan putting some new comics on the shelves. He was funny.

As soon as we got everything we needed, we went to the cashier to pay for the comics. The clerk asked us some questions.

"Oh hey there, Bubs." The clerk said, "What did you get today?"

"Well we got some of those interesting comics that just came today and we want to know how much those things cost." I replied.

"Yeah." Butchie chimed in.

The clerk checked the comics and added the money together like in math class years ago. "That will be $40.00."

I gave him my credit card and he was asking us about the superhero team in the comic book. He thought that they sound interesting.

"Pretty much," I replied. "Yeah."

Butchie nodded, "Me too."

"Well just between you and me," the clerk whispered, "I'm actually one of them."

"Okay?!!!" Butchie and I replied awkwardly.

The clerk finished and gave us our bags, "Well we gotta go now," I said. "Thanks for ringing us up." The whole situation was really awkward. Did he really think we believed he was a superhero?

"Yeah." Butchie said, "Thanks, pal."

"Come again, Bubs." The clerk said as we left the counter.

"Shesh," I whispered to Butchie, "Can you believe that guy?"

"I know, Right?" Butchie replied, "What a weirdo!"

After Butchie and I were done paying for the comics, I saw Sammy and her little brother Mikey trying to pick out some comic books.

I told Butchie, "That's the girl I was talking about last night."

Butchie suggested that I should ask her out. I was afraid that I might say the wrong words if I talked to her. She might reject me because she might have a boyfriend already or she might not be the dating kind or she doesn't have time for boys right now or she just sees me as a friend.

Butchie asked, "What's wrong, man?"

"I'm not sure I can do this, Butchie." I whispered to Butchie, "I mean what if she says no. Besides I can ask her when I want to."

Suddenly, a voice from behind me said, "Shorty?"

Sammy and I were happy to see each other. We shook hands. I introduced Butchie to Sammy. We asked her what she is doing at the comic book store. She explained to me that she was helping Mikey pick up some comics. Sammy introduced us to Mikey. He was too shy to talk to new people. I'd rather not bother him too much and I nervously asked her if she had any plans either this weekend or sometime soon. Surprisingly, she said she was free. I was thrilled.

"So, Sammy." I asked her, "When would be a good time for us to get together?"

Sammy responded, "Well I'm free on Friday."

"I was thinking about going to a restaurant and a movie with a bunch of people and hope you could join us." I told her, "How's that sound?"

Sammy accepted. I asked her where she lives and she responded, "29 Cooper Street 3D."

She asked me, "So what time would you guys come?"

I responded, "How about 7?"

Once again, she agreed, "Sounds great, Shorty."

Sammy asked me if Mikey can come because she didn't want him to be left out.

I responded, "Of course."

As soon as Sammy and I said goodbye to each other, I turned towards Butchie happily.

"Well there you go, man." Butchie said, "You got yourself a lucky lady."

We gave each other a high 5. I thanked Butchie for helping me ask Sammy on a date.

"Hey, you know what they say, pal?" Butchie responded, "You have a little help from your best buddy." We walked out of the comic book store, and went back home.

Although we did not see them, Victor and Billy were behind a rack in the comic book store. They saw me talking to Sammy and they were shocked that she accepted my invitation.

Victor stated to Billy, "We need to report this to Shark immediately."

They tried to get out of the rack, but they accidentally knocked it down along with the comics. The comic book clerk was freaked out as Victor and Billy ran off. The Hamilton Brothers left the comic book store to find Shark.

The two brothers exited the Uptown Comics and looked around for a way to follow. There were no cabs in sight, but Billy noticed a car parked next to the store. The keys were in the car, so Billy jumped in and started it up. "Let's go, Victor," he shouted. Victor walked over quickly. "Are you sure you want to steal a car, Billy?" he asked. "What steal?" Billy responded. "I'm…borrowing it. Yeah, that's what I'm doing. I'm borrowing it." The two drove off in the car.

The car was low on gas, so first they stopped to fill up. As always, they fought, this time about who would fill the car. They were both doing a tug of war with the gas until they accidentally threw it, hitting a random guy on the head, knocking him unconscious, much to the Hamilton Brothers' shock. Victor looked at Billy. "Dude," he said, "that's not good…at all! Let's get outta here!" The two jumped in the car, Billy still behind the wheel, and took off.

The two intended to follow me so that they could report back to Shark. However, Billy is a terrible driver, and easily distracted, and in a few blocks they crashed the car into a wall. Victor jumped out, bleeding from a cut on his face. "You idiot," he yelled at his brother. "You almost got me killed! That is probably the stupidest thing you've ever done!"

"Don't sell me short," Billy responded. "I've done much stupider things than that. Remember the time I…"

"NOT NOW YOU MORON!" Victor roared. "We need to get outta here!" Billy stumbled out of the car and they took off on foot just as a crowd was starting to gather. They were gone just a moment when a young guy, the clerk from the comic book store, ran up. "MY CAR!" he exclaimed, tears welling up. "MY…BEAUTIFUL…CAR."

****

Butchie and I went back to our apartment to tell my Mom the big news about Sammy saying she would go out with me. Cinnamon is barking out of excitement. It annoyed Mom, because she was talking to somebody on the phone.

As soon as Mom hung up, she asked me "What's the big news?"

I responded, "Butchie and I saw Sammy at Uptown Comics and I asked her if she wants to come out with all of us Friday at 7."

"Shorty!" Mom complained, "I told you that Sammy is not your girlfriend, she's your community habilitation worker! That means she's supposed to help you learn independent living skills, not be your girlfriend."

"Mom!" I replied, "Butchie and I just bumped into her at the Uptown Comics and started talking. We also met her little brother, Mikey, today and he is going to join us too."

Although Mom was happy for me, she warned me that you need to be careful who you ask out. She said the girl might already have a boyfriend, or she'll turn out cold, or just want to see me as a friend or client. I felt like she was trying to ruin the moment.

"But Mom, I'm not in love with her." I complained to her, "We're just hanging out. Besides, she's my friend. I can hang out with whoever I want!"

My mother doesn't like it when people yell at her. She said, "You don't have to be nasty to me, Shorty!"

I responded, "Sorry, Mom. I can be frustrated sometimes."

"It's OK, Sweetie. Now what day and time are you and your friends going out?"

I responded, "Friday at 7." She wrote it on the schedule.

****

Meanwhile, Sammy and Mikey came back home to 29 Cooper Street 3D and their grandmother, Joan Johnson, was in the kitchen cooking dinner for them.

Mikey was teasing his big sister about her "boyfriend" and Sammy was annoyed. She corrected him, saying that I'm not her boyfriend. I'm just her client and her friend. Joan asked Sammy what they're yelling about.

Mikey responded, "Sammy's got a boyfriend!"

Sammy groaned as Mikey laughs.

"Mikey, mind your manners!" Joan said as she turned to Sammy. "Now Sammy, who's Shorty?"

Sammy responded, "He's this guy I met at the meeting yesterday in my training to be a therapist and I'm helping him. I saw him at Uptown Comics with his friend today and he invited me and Mikey to a restaurant and a movie on Friday at 7."

Joan was happy for her and asked Sammy if I had anything to do with Shark, because she didn't like the way Shark treated her. She's glad Sammy decided to break up with him. Sammy had not even told her grandmother about Shark coming to the apartment building with a necklace. She didn't want to worry her grandmother.

Annoyed, Sammy asked as she sighed, "Oh Nana, why are you bringing Shark into this?"

Joan responded, "I'm just afraid and worried he might be another pig like that Shark, my dear."

Sammy tearfully stormed off to her room. Joan felt bad about mentioning Shark. Sammy was crying and cried even harder when she saw a picture of herself and her parents. She is secretly a depressed young woman still recovering from the deaths of her parents. Joan overheard Sammy crying and decided to give her some time alone.

"The poor dear," she thought. "Oh she must be suffering even more than I realized."

****

Later that night, Victor called Shark from the room he shared with Billy.

When he told Shark about Sammy going out with another guy, Shark slammed down the phone yelling, "Son of a..."

Victor hung up and he said, "I think this is gonna get ugly."

"Looking at you, man," Billy responded. "It looks like it already has."

Victor asked, "What is that supposed to mean?"

Billy responded, "It means you're ugly."

Victor yelled, "No, you're ugly!"

He punched Billy in the face and they both fell onto the ground. Their mother came in. "What's all the commotion?" They ignored her.

Mrs. Hamilton yelled, "BOYS!!"

She beat them with a broom so they would stop fighting. Mrs. Hamilton ordered the boys to do 50 pushups to calm down.

Their mother, Sharon Hamilton is caring toward her sons and loves them a whole bunch. However, despite this, she is extremely strict whenever Victor and Billy do something they're not supposed to do. She has blonde-gray hair, wears rounded glasses. She is considerably shorter than Billy and Victor, but she is a tough woman and you do not want to mess with her. She has a military background and always runs a tight ship. Their mother is very intelligent. Sharon has issues with her argumentative husband. They argue so much they did not realize that their two sons, who are not the sharpest tools in the shed, are hanging out with a twisted psychopath.

****

Meanwhile, Shark was heading toward Sammy's apartment door. He doesn't seem too happy when he thinks about Sammy going out with another guy. When Shark knocked, Sammy thought her grandmother must have gone out and forgotten her key.

She opened the door without asking who's there. She was freaked out to see Shark standing there.

Shark started questioning her about dating some other guy. "Who is this rat you're going out with?"

Sammy responded that it's none of his business and she wondered how he even knew what she was doing.

"Hey, you don't get to choose!! I choose!!" Shark said as he attempted to grab her by the wrist.

She grabbed the pepper spray on the hall table, sprayed him in the face, and slammed the door. Shark was enraged and vowed to find the man who is "separating" them. He wanted to separate Sammy from the other guy, even if it was the last thing he did, and no one was going to stop him.

****

The next day at Blockbuster, I was gathering some returned videos and putting them on shelves. I was daydreaming about Sammy in my Romeo and Juliet fantasy.

When I was dreaming that Sammy and I were about to kiss, my fantasy Sammy yelled in a weird voice, "HOPKINS!!!!!"

I woke up when I actually heard, "HOPKINS!!!!!" It was my grouchy, cantankerous, hot-tempered, and loudmouthed boss and neighbor Old Man Edward, who also lived in the apartment a floor below mine. I always drove him crazy. When I sing and dance, jump up and down, I always drive him completely insane. It's kind of like Dennis the Menace did to Mr. Wilson. He also reminded me of one of those funny cartoon managers of the places where the protagonists like Superman or Spider-Man or Fred Flintstones or George Jetson work, sort of like Perry White, J. Jonah Jameson, Cosmo Spacely and Mr. Slate.

"Why are you lollygagging?" Old Man Edward yelled, "GET TO WORK!!!!"

I responded, "Y-Yes, sir."

"Sheesh, Hopkins." Old Man Edward complained, "One of these days, I'll end up in a mental hospital!"

"Sheesh, I feel like I've been bossed around by a parrot," I thought to myself. "That's exactly what he sounds like."

My co-worker, Ernie Anderson asked me, "What was that all about?"

Ernie is a good friend of mine and also happens to be my teacher's son. He understands that I get distracted sometimes.

"Were you daydreaming again?" he asked.

I responded, "Yeah, there is a girl that I'm dreaming about dating and I can't get her out of my mind."

Ernie asked me, "Oooooo, who's the lucky lady?"

"Well her name is Sammy Johnson." I explained to Ernie, "She's helping me socialize. You know like going to places without having my mother around, blah, blah, blah!"

"Good for you." Ernie responded with a giggle. "I'm glad you're being an MRA."

That's a catchy way to say mature and responsible adult. I told Ernie that he was starting to sound like my mother because she uses that phrase all the time. I always remember catchy statements from other people.

The next "customers" came in. It was Shark and his cronies, Victor and Billy. I didn't even know I was in danger when these jerks came in. It's like a western movie where the fearsome villain barges into the saloon.

Victor spotted me putting movies on shelves and said to Shark. "There he is, man, the guy who asked your girl out."

Repulsed by my appearance and enraged, Shark said, "That *retard* is dead-meat. Come on."

Shark came toward me, grabbed me by my shirt and slammed me towards the wall near the video shelves and I said, "Welcome to Blockbuster and what can I..."

"SILENCE!!!" Shark yelled and he coldly asked me, "Do you have any idea who I am?"

I responded, "Um, wait... err, um... don't tell me, um..."

"Don't answer!!" Shark interrupted me as he snarled, "I'm called Jack "Shark" Roderick, a dangerous predator to any mistakes God made like you. What's your name, *Retard*?" I thought to myself, "Why would he say that? Only an ignorant, treacherous villain would use the R word. What a monster he must be."

"S...S...Shorty Hopkins?" I responded in a nervous frightened voice, "W...W...Why do you ask?"

"Listen to me, Hopkins," Shark responded with a sneer on his face. "You stay away from my angel, Samantha Johnson. Do you hear?"

I was really confused. Is Sammy dating somebody else? She had not said anything, and I didn't know what the story was.

"Well I didn't know you're dating her," I replied. "You see I've been asking girls out, but..."

"SHUT UP!!!!" Shark shouted. "You don't come near my girl again because if you do, I'll crucify you."

I giggled at first because I didn't understand what he meant by that, but the word "crucify" sounded like a funny word. Before I could talk, Shark once again threatened me as he pulled me closer to him with a snarl on his face.

"I think I'm going to wet myself, Dude." Billy nervously whimpered to Victor.

Victor whispered out of the corner of his mouth. "Billy." He actually didn't want Billy to get hurt because Shark had ordered them to not speak unless they're spoken to. For a bossy and crazy guy like me, that's pretty cruel, isn't it?

"Listen up, Hopkins. We got a way of doing' things here in this world. We all make mistakes, even God, and I'm staring at one of God's mistakes right now. To me, *retards* like you always look like something the animal spit up. I'm Adam and Samantha is my Eve. We are destined to be one. Some people probably know better than to take what isn't theirs and like I said before, she is my Eve. So if you see her again, talk to her again, or even think of her again, I'll burn your house down with you and your family in it, UNDERSTAND?!"

I was so frightened. I responded, "Y-yes, sir."

"Good boy," Shark said sadistically as he put me down.

"Come on guys," Shark said with a hideous laugh, "Let's get out of this *retard* convention."

The Hamilton Brothers felt badly for me deep down while Shark felt good about insulting me and using the "R" word on me.

As soon as the guys left, Ernie comforted me, "Are you all right, Shorty?"

I responded softly, "Yeah. That was pretty scary."

He warned me about this monster. Ernie explained that Shark is a bigoted, racist, sexist and homophobic fool. He told me how Shark made fun of Ernie one time because Ernie is gay. Then he beat up Ernie and his partner, Gary.

Shark thinks he is God's perfect child since he is a religious fanatic. No one knows why he is so hateful. It is certainly not how his religion would want someone to act.

"Didn't you tell anybody?" I asked Ernie. "Did you call the police?"

Ernie said no because Shark threatened that he would hunt him down and kill him like an animal. Ernie believed Shark is capable of anything.

"Beware of him, Shorty. You do not want to cross him. He is really crazy." Ernie warned me again and I was worried Shark would hurt me.

As I was about to ask Ernie another question, Old Man Edward showed up from the other side of the store and shouted, "What's going on here?!"

We both responded, "Nothing, sir."

"Well stop doing nothing and GET BACK TO WORK OR YOU'RE BOTH FIRED!!!" Sullivan yelled, "GO!! GO!! GOOOOOO!!!!!" Old Man Edward yelled in his parrot voice.

As soon as we got back to work, I thought about what Ernie had said. I was scared by Shark's threat and even Ernie thought I had every reason to be scared. He might kill me in a matter of time. It's like a monstrous boogeyman coming out of the closet, or under the bed, or something like that. This time though the threat is real.

I was asking myself, "How am I going to tell Sammy?"

I was so scared when Shark blasted me and ordered me to stay away from Sammy. He has no right to decide what Sammy and I should do or not do. I mean seriously. Sometimes, I boss people around and I hate being told what to do. What a complete jerk!! I'm really scared, but I still want to hang out with Sammy. Oh what to do, what to do? Oh great, now I'm starting to sound like Winnie the Pooh. Sometimes whenever Pooh doesn't know what to do, he just sits on a big log and he always asks himself, "Oh what to do, what to do?"

Anyway, let's just get to the next scene of the story.

****

Meanwhile, Sammy was hanging out with her friend Maureen Myllek at the mall. They were eating lunch and Maureen asked Sammy what she thought about her new clothes she was wearing.

"I don't know," Sammy responded. "I like the outfit, but I think the boots look too big on you."

She asked her if she had any plans on Friday night around 7:00. Sammy told her that she already had plans. "Remember this guy I was telling you about, Shorty?"

Maureen responded, "Yeah, how short is he?"

"Actually, he's pretty tall," Sammy said. "He invited me to the movies."

Maureen said, "Really? Is he cute?"

Sammy asked, "You know Brad Pitt?"

Maureen responded, "Yeah?"

Sammy stated, "Well he's not like him. LOL He looks fine though."

Caitlin Oliver showed up on her lunch break from the Fashion Bug and joined their conversation.

She complimented Maureen on her purchase, saying, "I really like your new dress."

Suddenly, Sammy's long time rival who is rich, famous and popular, Angelica "Angie" Elizabeth and her tall, handsome, successful, but haughty boyfriend, Peter Dreggs showed up.

Angie asked, "What's up girlfriends?!"

Sammy and her friends sighed as Sammy responded, "What do you want, Angie?"

"Guess what?" Angie asked. "You girls know my boyfriend, right? We're just doing a little shopping." Sammy got annoyed because it made her think of Shark. Angie snickered. "Where's your boyfriend, Johnson? Did he find a new girlfriend or is he in jail? I thought you guys make a great couple."

Maureen yelled, "Hey, you want to back up that attitude, Angie?!"

Caitlin agreed with her. "Yeah, Angie! What has Sammy ever done to you?"

"Sheesh, calm down, Ladies," Angie responded. "I'm just saying hello."

Caitlin warned Angie that she would give her something to complain about if she continues to bother Sammy.

Angie responded as she walked off, "Whatever you say, weirdoes."

Dreggs said, "We wouldn't be caught dead with you people."

As Angie and Dreggs left, the girls went back to the table and comforted Sammy. "Listen, girl." said Caitlin. "Don't listen to what she has to say."

"Yeah, Sammy!" Maureen responded. "You ought to kick her into next week."

"No, violence is not my style." Sammy said, "God, this is a nightmare. Shark is a monster and then I have to listen to Angie make insulting comments. Why don't all the rotten people out there just disappear?"

Caitlin reminded Sammy, "Sammy, I know everything seems hopeless right now. But don't listen to fools like Angie. You have so much going for you. No one pays attention to a shrew like Angie."

"She's right, Sammy," Maureen nodded. "Don't let a twit like Angie get under your skin. And don't listen to what she says. Listen to me—I know everything, and I certainly know what's right for you!"

Sammy smirked. "Yeah," she answered sarcastically, "I'll listen to you."

****

Later that night while Mom was talking with a friend on the phone and doing paperwork, Butchie and Stephanie came through the door. They had a blast at a party at Fordham.

They were laughing as Stephanie said, "I can't believe how much that guy drank! He must have had 50 beers. He couldn't walk."

"I know!" Butchie replied. "He was bumping into everything. Don't people know they should stop drinking before they get to that point? Some people just don't know their limits."

"Will you two quiet down?" Mom said. "I'm trying to hear my friend on the phone."

Stephanie said, "Sorry, Betty." She whispered to Butchie, "I hope Betty's not mad at us. I didn't realize she was on the phone."

"No, of course not," Butchie replied. "She's just trying to hear someone on the phone. I'm sure we were just being too loud and she couldn't hear the person on the phone."

Stephanie smiled and said, "I know. We were pretty loud."

Butchie leaned over and wanted to give Stephanie a romantic kiss, but I came home feeling depressed. I just wanted to go to my room, not eat, not talk, nothing. Cinnamon once again barked out of excitement. Mom got off the phone and was concerned when she saw me. She wanted Butchie and Stephanie to go talk to me.

I was sitting on my bed, still traumatized by Shark's threat. I heard a knock on the door.

"Who's there?" I called.

It was Butchie and Stephanie, calling behind the door. "It's us, Shorty!" Stephanie called.

"Yeah, we just want to make sure you're okay, pal." Butchie called.

I didn't open the door, but I told them about Shark's threatening me at Blockbuster earlier. I also told them about Shark telling me I could not see Sammy again and how he ordered me to stay away from her. Shocked and disturbed by this, Butchie and Stephanie were trying to comfort me, but I was shaking.

"Where did this guy get off threatening me?" I asked. "He doesn't own Sammy anymore than I do."

"Yeah!!" Butchie responded. "You're absolutely right, pal. You ought to set him straight."

"Uhh...Butchie," I said. "How am I going to do that?! He's got a gun."

"Ohh, well good luck with that." Butchie replied.

"Listen, Shorty," Stephanie said. "You don't have to listen to what some psycho has to say and you can talk to Sammy whenever you want. You can't let some bully push you around. He has no right."

I was thinking about it and realized that Stephanie is absolutely right. "I can talk to Sammy if I want to and if I want to go out with her and if she wants to go out with me, that's too bad!" I puff up my chest and I feel like a superhero right now. I continued, "Besides, we're still going to see the movie and nothing is going to stop us. She's also my community habilitation worker so she has to spend time with me!" I also made a conclusion, "Besides, time is better than force!"

****

On Friday evening, Victor and Billy were walking on the sidewalk. Billy was eating donuts, his favorite food, and Victor was finishing his favorite food, a "vegan" donut.

"God," Billy said with his mouth full, "those donuts are SO good."

"Oh tell me about it, dude," Victor replied. "Can this day get any better?"

Victor spotted a young woman. He pulled Billy's shirt and pointed, "Dude, look at that amazing girl."

Billy also was attracted to her, "Oh my God, she's so hot. Come on."

"Wait!!" Victor said as he pulled his shirt and whispered, "Just follow my lead, man."

They went up to her and Victor said, "Hey, nice body, babe." It shocked and angered her. She turned around and said nicely, "Come here."

His face got close. He closed his eyes and puckered up. She punched him between the eyes.

As Victor fell to the ground in agony. Billy said with his mouth full, "I'm not with this guy."

She stormed off.

Victor got up just as I was leaving the video store... Victor asked, "Hey, isn't that the guy that Shark is always talking about?"

Billy responded with his mouth full, "Wh... What guy?"

Victor pointed, "That guy right there."

Billy looked in my direction and then exclaimed with his mouth full, "Uhh...I don't know."

Annoyed, Victor stated, "Mommy really did damage to you when she dropped you on your head as a baby."

Billy replied. "Wow, lucky guess, man."

Victor thought they should start their look out.

They saw me as I went into the phone booth and dialed Sammy's number. Sammy was sitting down brushing her hair and the phone rang. She picked up the phone on top of her desk and said, "Hello."

I responded, "Hi Sammy."

Sammy asked, "Do you have any plans for tonight?"

I responded sarcastically, "Why do you ask questions which you already know the answer to?"

She chuckled as I said, "Actually, me and the guys are going out for pizza and going to the movies and I was wondering if you could come."

Sammy responded, "Shorty, you already asked me that question a few days ago and I said yes."

I quoted from Snow White, "Oh...gosh!!"

Sammy giggled and said, "Well are you a Bashful fella?"

I responded, "Yeah, I'm a regular wallflower."

A voice yelled from outside of her room. "Sammy!"

"Coming, Nana! I gotta go, Shorty," Sammy responded. "I'll see you later."

"Sure thing, Sammy," I responded. "Bye!" We hung up and I got out of the phone booth.

What I didn't know was that Victor and Billy were watching me the whole time while I was talking to Sammy on the phone. I thought they were waiting for me to get out of the phone booth.

"It's all yours." I said as I turned and walked away.

They thought they should spy on me in case anything happened that they should report to Shark about Sammy and me.

While they were trying to follow me, Victor unexpectedly tripped on a curb. Billy continued walking, and laughed, but slipped on a banana peel that someone had littered on the sidewalk and fell to the ground, much to his surprise.

Luckily, neither was injured, even though Billy had trouble getting up because he slipped on the banana peel a second time as he tried to get up.

"Dude," Billy said to Victor, laughing at his misfortune, "That was awesome! Do that again!"

Annoyed, Victor yelled, "Just shut up!!!"

Billy responded as he ran up to him and pulled him up, "OK! OK! OK!"

As Victor glared at Billy, he asked, "What?"

He asked softly, "Were you born yesterday?!"

"I don't know," Billy responded. "why?"

"Well in case you haven't noticed," Victor complained, "I just tripped on a curb. I coulda broken my neck!!!!"

Billy responded, "So."

Annoyed, Victor shook his head, "Whatever! Let's just go."

Billy thought to himself as he ran with Victor, "Wow, what a jerk." Those guys are pretty silly clowns, huh?

****

Sammy helped her grandma carry her laundry upstairs while Mikey snuck into her room and read her diary.

When his sister returned, she yelled, "Hey, that's my diary! Get away from it!"

"If you want it," Mikey teased. "you'll have to catch me!"

As they were running through the room, Joan spotted them and ordered the kids to stop running and told Mikey to hand the diary back to Sammy.

Mikey responded, as he gave the diary back to his sister, "Oh alright."

After Mikey left, Joan asked her granddaughter if she was ready for her romantic date.

"Nana, it's not a date." Sammy reminded her grandmother, "Shorty was only asking me and Mikey to hang out with him and some of his friends. His mother and her friend are even coming. Does that seem very romantic to you?"

Joan was still concerned about Sammy's "date" because she was afraid that I might turn out like Shark. Sammy got annoyed and went back to her room with her diary to get ready for the big night.

Joan thought to herself, "That girl had better be careful."

****

I met my mother, Butchie and Stephanie outside of our apartment. Diane couldn't make it tonight because she has a very important meeting. We all walked to Sammy and Mikey's apartment to go out for pizza. I introduced Sammy to Stephanie.

"This is my boyfriend Butchie." Stephanie said as she put her arm around Butchie.

"I already met Butchie." Sammy replied.

"Oh yeah?" Stephanie asked. "Well back off!!!" Sammy looked a little surprised by Stephanie's reaction, but started talking to my mother.

Mom didn't like Stephanie's tone with Sammy, although she understands that Stephanie has this jealousy issue when it comes to Butchie and other women. Stephanie and Mom met Mikey, Sammy's little brother. I wanted to talk to Sammy, but Mom and Sammy were having a good conversation so I decided not to chime in.

We went to Smokey Jones' Pizza. What we don't know is that Victor and Billy had followed us without even being seen. They didn't see where I live yet because they were both distracted by a young woman. Unfortunately for them, the Hamilton Brothers didn't have a reservation. The host named TexLex ordered them to leave. Billy tried to sneak in, but the host prevented them from entering. Victor put his foot out, tripped TexLex, which caused him to fall and lose consciousness. His full name is Lex Lewis, but he nicknamed himself "TexLex" in order to sound cool. Not only does TexLex greet customers, but he likes to light up candles to make the tables fancy for them.

Together, the Hamilton Brothers put the unconscious TexLex into a closet and snuck into the restaurant without anybody noticing.

"Wow," Sammy said, "This place looks beautiful. I wasn't expecting such a nice place when you said we were going to go to a pizza restaurant."

"Not bad, huh?" I replied. "This is one of my favorite places to go out for dinner."

"Yeah," Butchie chimed in. "It is."

"Well I gotta tell you guys," Sammy said "This place is fabulous."

We also met a funny hysterical waiter. A waiter said, "Good evening, folks! Welcome to "Smokey Jones." My name is Kevin Jones and I will..."

Suddenly, there was some loud noise coming from the kitchen. "What in tarnation is that noise?" I said in a southern accent.

It continued until some guy came crashing through the swinging door to the kitchen, crashing into Kevin so that the two of them were knocked to the floor

The two got up and the crazy nut job shouted out, "HELLO, CUSTOMERS!!!!!" Kevin looked really annoyed with him, "IIIIIIIIIIIIIIIIIIIIIII'M TED!!!"

"Ted! How many times do I have to tell you," Kevin shouted, "YOU DON'T WORK HERE?!"

"Of course I work here!!" Ted responded. "Because I love to show friendly service to a bunch of LOSERS!!"

Kevin shouted, "JUST GET OF HERE BEFORE I CALL THE COPS!!!!"

"AAWW!!!!" Ted said in a disappointed tone, "you ain't fun no more, Kev."

As Ted exited the door, Kevin sighed and said, "As I was saying, I will be taking care of you tonight."

As I raised my hand, Mom reminded me, "Shorty, this is not a school."

Kevin claimed that it's okay. "What can I get you, sir?"

As I was about to order my drink, Ted came bursting through the door and sang out loud, "LA! LA! LA! LA! TED IS BACK IN TOWN!! TED IS BACK IN TOWN!! YEAH!!!!"

Kevin once again shouted out, "TED!!! I TOLD YOU TO GET OUT OF HERE!!!!"

Ted hysterically replied, "WELL I JUST HEARD THAT THIS YOUNG MAN HERE WANTED TO GET A DRINK! SO WHAT CAN I GET FOR YOU, SON?"

When I ordered the drinks I wanted, Ted hysterically yelled, "You want a drink of water and apple juice, huh!"

I responded awkwardly, "Uh...yeah."

"Well ask me if I care!!" Ted said to me in a crazy voice, "Go ahead, boy! Ask me if I care!! ASK ME IF I CARE!!!!"

"Okay," I responded awkwardly. "Uhh...do you care?"

Ted calmly stated as he came towards me, "Let me see." He leans down and yells in my ear, "NOOOOOOOOOO!!!" His yelling was so loud, I fell off the chair.

As I was getting back to my chair, Mikey used a hardwood slingshot on Ted with a piece of bread and hit him. The hit caused Ted to smash into the other table. Sammy was mad at Mikey for doing that.

"Mikey!" Sammy yelled, "How could you do that?"

Sammy wanted Mikey to apologize to Ted, but Ted got up and yelled, "What's wrong with you, boy? I ain't no target for a carnival game!!"

Mikey responded, "It was fun."

"You really think that's funny," Ted complains. "don't you, boy?!!!!"

Mikey replied, "Yes."

"Well let me tell you something you little piece of the devil!!" Ted yelled, picking Mikey up in the air, "Nobody targets Ted and if anybody messes with Ted, punks like you are making a big mista..."

Sammy smacked Ted in the head with her purse to save her brother from Ted. A drowsy Ted finished his sentence as he fell, "mistake." Seriously, I feel like I'm in one of those cartoon sketches if you know what I mean.

As soon as Kevin finished taking our orders, he dragged a disoriented Ted into a different location. What Kevin doesn't know is that he put Ted in the same storage closet TexLex was in after the Hamilton Brothers knocked him out.

"Excuse me, young man!" a woman shouted. "I need some service over here!!"

"I'll be right there, ma'am." Kevin replied. Although he is annoyed with her bossy behavior, he knows he has to wait on her. He has to bring my table's order first. Besides, Kevin always gets overwhelmed by the woman's particularly complicated orders.

****

Meanwhile, Victor and Billy sat a few tables away from us. Victor looked through the hole in his taquito like a telescope to spy on us. Billy looked straight into the side of his donut. Unsurprisingly, he cannot see a thing, though Billy wonders why that is, which annoys Victor. He reminds Billy there's a hole in the middle of a donut.

Billy is unable to see through the holes of his donuts and is unable to see us. He thinks the sun is pink and frosty and then calls it beautiful.

Annoyed, Victor asked Billy, "You really haven't got any brains at all, have you, Billy?"

"Yes," Billy replied, "How do you know that, Vic?"

"Oh give me that." Victor grabbed the donut from Billy.

"Hey!" Billy yelled.

Victor pointed at the hole in the middle of the donut. "Oooooohhhhhh!!!! I get you now."

Suddenly, the Hamilton Brothers spotted a beautiful girl by herself. They argue until Billy challenges Victor: both of them will get a chance to sit down and start a conversation with the girl. "She can choose," Billy says. "She's gonna choose me," Victor answered.

First Billy walked over. "Hi," he said. "I'm Billy. May I sit down?"

The woman shakes her head vehemently. "No," she says in a loud, clear voice.

"Why, thank you," Billy responds as he pulls the chair out and sits down. He starts into his monologue, speaking in a low voice so Victor could not hear him. He spoke for only a moment before the woman stood up, shouted "How dare you?" and slapped Billy hard across the face, knocking him to the floor. The woman then stormed off as Victor laughed and Billy lay on the floor, whimpering.

It was several minutes before the woman returned, just enough time for Billy to crawl back to his table while Victor mocked him. She sat down, and Victor looked dismissively at his brother. "Baby brother," he said, "let me show you how it's done." With that, he stood up and walked calmly over to her table.

"Hi," he said smoothly. "I'm Victor. Can I take a seat?"

"I really prefer to be left alone," she answered, at least a little annoyed.

"Why, thank you," Victor responded, obviously not listening to her. She, however, had had enough. She stood up as Victor was sitting down. "I SAID NO!" she roared as she threw a glass of water in his face and then walloped him with an open hand. Victor was crying before he hit the floor, and the women left the restaurant as fast as she could.

Victor finally stopped crying, got up and walked back to his table. He plopped down in his chair, and looked defeatedly at his brother. "So," Billy said, "who won?"

Victor glares at Billy.

"What?" Billy asked in confusion. "What did I say?"

Lesson Learned: Don't be a jerk. There are better ways to get a girlfriend...or boyfriend. Be patient, kind, gentle, sweet, charming, and appreciate that person. Show respect and love, not possessive and obsessive love, but an emotional sense of love. Just be friends with that person and give that person time. If you and your friend decide to get together, go for it. If your friend doesn't love you in return, respect his or her choice to remain friends. Don't be creepy.

****

Moments later, Kevin arrived with our pizza and placed it on our table. "Pizza time, everyone!! Who is ready for some of the best pizza in town?" Kevin put two large pizzas on the table: one plain, one with sausage and meatball on it.

Sammy looked at the bounty on the table, and smiled. "Just what I expected," she said. "One plain, one meatball and sausage."

I looked at her and smiled back. "I wouldn't have my Friday any other way," I said. "Except that it's one plain, one sausage and meatball."

"I better write that down," Sammy answered. "That way I will get them in the right order."

We had a wonderful meal together, laughing and talking into the night, including ice cream for dessert. That was Mikey's favorite part.

****

Meanwhile, Victor and Billy were still spying on us. They watched the whole meal, all the while continuing their amazingly idiotic conversation and fighting with one another.

"I wish we had people that care about us like that guy that we are watching does," Billy said. "That's really nice."

"Nice?" Victor shot back. "You idiot! We do have people who care about us! They are our parents! Remember our parents?"

"Uhhhhhh, what?" was the best that Billy could manage.

"Our parents! Mom and Dad!" Victor exclaimed. "Man…you really did fall down the stairs and bang your head as a child again and again, didn't you?"

"Uhhhhh. I think so," Billy responded. "At least, that's what Mom told me, Vic."

Victor stands and spreads his arms out like he is making a big announcement, "Ladies and Gentlemen," he said. "My brother the idiot!"

By then Billy has lost his focus and was distracted by the fact that the pepper shaker seemed to be clogged. He picked it up, looked inside, shook it violently, and tried it. Still no luck. He looked inside again, put his mouth over the holes in the shaker, and blew as hard as he could. The pepper, ground to a fine powder, exploded upward and into his face.

"OH MY GOD!" Billy roared. "MY EYES…MY EYES! I can't see!" His eyes were tearing as if he was crying, and stung terribly. "IT HURTS, VIC. IT HURTS!"

Victor got some water and poured it into his eyes to flush them out, but Billy continued to cry and complain. A waitress came over to see if he needed help. "Does he need help? An ambulance?" she asked. "No," Victor says. "He could use some common sense though."

****

As we finished our dinner, the karaoke was about to start. Butchie and I went on stage and sang. Stephanie cheered us on while Sammy was sitting there, amazed how well we all sang together. As soon as the song ended, everyone cheered for us.

I explained to Sammy that just because we like to sing doesn't mean that I'm always good at it. We always like to do these things for fun. Sammy chuckles as she agrees with me. I asked her if she could sing. She responded, as she shook her head, "No."

The Hamilton Brothers were surprised when we sang karaoke and that the "guy who is hitting on Shark's girl" can sing. Victor and Billy were arguing and fighting over which of them is the better singer. They attracted everyone's attention while they threw food at each other. Mom ordered me not to get involved.

Suddenly, the owner of the restaurant named Louis "Smokey" Jones, who happens to be Kevin's grandfather, ordered the Hamilton Brothers to stop. Just then, the angry TexLex woke up and came out of the closet.

"They did it, Smokey!!" TexLex shouted. "They knocked me out, put me in the closet, and trespassed inside your restaurant!"

The boys got thrown out into the dumpster by Jones and TexLex. They put him into the closet earlier…oh wait I already said that, sorry.

"AND STAY OUT!!!" Jones shouted in complete anger. "DON'T EVEN COME BACK, YOU CRAZY BUFFOONS!!!!" Jones slammed the door. His voice sounded like Darth Vader from the Star Wars Trilogy.

Everybody, including me, was asking about those two weirdos. Sammy immediately figured out who they were, but she didn't want to talk about it and pretended she didn't know them because of Shark. I asked if she was OK.

Sammy responded, "I'm fine, Shorty."

Mom checked her watch and realized that it was time to go to the movies. We all got up from the table, paid the bill and left.

****

In the alleyway, Victor and Billy got out of the dumpster with flies flying all around them. The boys were breathing heavily and they both smelled really bad, much to their horror.

"Ugh, Billy." Victor said, "You smell like garbage."

Billy responded, "No, you LOOK like garbage!"

Victor thinks it was all Billy's fault, but Billy disagrees and slaps Victor. Victor slapped Billy back, but that just made him complain about his ruined bowl haircut. Billy tried to punch him, but Victor ran away from him.

They were once again fighting until they saw Sammy, Mom, my friends, and me walking into the movie theater. The theater looked beautiful because of the lights on the building. I told Sammy that I honestly think that it's like an early Christmas tree. Mom asked the movie clerk for the movie tickets.

She gave them tickets and said, "Enjoy the show."

As we entered the theater, Victor and Billy arrived after they got out of the dumpster. Victor was hitting on the theater clerk while he was asking her to let them in.

"Hey, Babe," Victor asked. "How would you like for us to pick you up later after our movie?"

The clerk refused to allow them inside because they smell so badly.

"I don't stink," Victor said, trying to defend himself. "My brother is the one who stinks."

Billy responded, "Do not."

Victor shouted back, "Do too!"

Billy shouted back, "Do not!"

Victor shouted back, "Do too!"

As they continued fighting, the clerk pressed the button under the desk. The security guard appeared, grabbed them by the shirts, and threw into the same dumpster, which caused the lock on the dumpster lid to lock.

"Oh God," Billy complained. "not that smell again!!!"

Victor shouted out, "Shut up and open the lid!!"

When the Hamilton Brothers tried to open the lid, they realized that the lid is locked after they got thrown out again.

Billy asked, "So what the hell do we do now?"

Victor thought they should wait inside the dumpster until we got out of the theater, much to Billy's horror, causing him to scream at the top of his lungs.

"OH MY GOD!!!" Billy screamed through the dumpster lid. "NNNNOOOOOOOOOOOOOOOOOOOOOOOOOOOOOOOOO OOOOOOOOOOOO!!!!"

****

Meanwhile in the movie theater, the movie was starting. It turned out to be the premiere of "Disney's Beauty and the Beast." We all know that movie. It's one of the greatest movies of all time.

The movie was really outstanding, beautiful, entertaining and romantic. One character was really funny and he made me smile and I enjoyed his song.

The female lead had the voice of an angel. That movie helped me understand a lot of things. I finally understood what my parents were talking about: Be friends with a girl and eventually when the time comes, you might fall in love.

The love song nearly made me cry. The main antagonist of the movie was really funny at the beginning, but eventually he became a sadistic monster who would do anything to get what he wants like trying to get the girl to be his trophy wife.

I heard about Stockholm syndrome. My parents said it's a disturbing condition that makes you feel sympathy towards your captor, but the girl's "syndrome" isn't bad because as we already know, the girl and the horrifying monster, who lived in the enchanted castle, had a rough start and they eventually got along and eventually fell in love with each other, with the help of the monster's friendly and funny animated object servants. Besides, everything did work out in the end. When the girl became the monster's prisoner, it's like a parent grounding their child.

We were all clapping at the end and I wanted to stay for the credits. Everybody else in the theater left except for Sammy, and me. Sammy was crying. Mikey, Butchie, Stephanie and Mom went out to the lobby. Mikey thought the movie was awesome and was chatting about it on his way out.

I asked Sammy, "Aren't happy endings great?"

Sammy responded, "Yeah they can be."

Sammy and I stayed for all the credits. I explained that when I looked at the end credits, I imagine myself falling without hitting the ground. It's like falling down the stairs. I keep slamming on top of the letters and I jump off the letters like I am jumping off a high diving board. Sammy did not laugh at me like a lot of people would have. She thought I had quite an imagination.

As we got up, I noticed we weren't alone in the theater. The actress who voiced the lead girl was right behind us. Her name is Paige O'Hara. She is also a Broadway actress from the shows I've seen and she has a beautiful voice. We were excited to meet her and each of us got her autograph. She is a really friendly person.

As we were slowly going downstairs, Sammy slipped off the last step. I caught her and we started to stare at each other for a moment.

"Um, Shorty." Sammy told me to let her go. "You can put me down now."

I replied, "Oh right, sorry." We felt awkward about it.

Suddenly, Mikey came back in and sang, "Shorty and Sammy sitting in a tree, K-I-S-S-I-N-G!"

Sammy glares, "Mikey!!!"

"First comes love. Then comes marriage. Then comes baby in the baby carriage."

While he finishes his rhyme, Sammy shouts out, "Stop it, Mikey! Stop it! Stop it!"

Mikey left to join the others. Thank God.

Sammy and I had a great conversation about the movie being dedicated to a guy named Howard Ashman, who created the lyrics for the movie, along with the songs for the other movies like:

"Disney's The Little Mermaid",

"Disney's Aladdin",

"Warner Bros' "Little Shop of Horrors" (1986) and (1982 musical)

"Kurt Vonnegut's "God Bless You, Mr. Rosewater",

"Smile" (musical),

"The Confirmation",

and "Disney's Oliver & Company."

I told Sammy how he also did the lyrics from an anti-drug video from last year, "Cartoon All-Stars to the Rescue," my favorite cartoon crossover of all time.

Right before I left the theater, I turned towards the screen, smirked and said "Thank you, Howard." Sammy said. "Gee, Shorty. You sure know a lot about this guy." We left the theater.

****

In the alleyway next to the theater, the dumpster lid opened a little bit. Victor and Billy wanted to follow us home from the theater so they could report back to Shark.

"Come on, Vic!" Billy complained. "We've been in this dumpster for nearly two hours. When will they...?"

Victor responded quietly, "Shh...They're coming."

They were going to open the lid, but unfortunately for them, the latch got stuck and they could not open the top. They forgot all about the lock.

We left the movie theater and were walking back home, talking about how awesome the movie was. We were all talking and I was picturing the movie in my head.

"So, Shorty," Sammy asked. "How did you like the movie?"

"It was something," I said. "It doesn't matter how old I am, I always enjoy movies no matter what they say."

"What are you talking about, Shorty?" Sammy asked. "People of all ages like movies."

"I know," I responded. "Sometimes I just don't make any sense whatsoever."

"Don't put yourself down," Sammy said. "Getting back to the movie, I believe it was phenomenal. It should win the Academy Award."

My mother, Mikey, Butchie and Stephanie agreed with her. Mikey shouted, "That was one of the best movies I've ever seen!!"

Mikey kept on talking about the movie and demonstrated the final battle and the songs from the movie. He made karate chops with his arms while he sang in a loud voice.

I secretly whispered to Sammy, "And they say I talk too much."

"I know Shorty." She smirked and nodded. "Sometimes my little brother is a genuine comedian."

When we got to Sammy and Mikey's apartment, we all wished them good night and Sammy thanked us for inviting them. As soon as she and Mikey entered the apartment building door, we headed home.

On the way home, Mom told me she had noticed that Sammy had a brutal mark on her arm. Mom asked me how I thought Sammy had gotten the bruise. It really concerned her. She had wanted to ask Sammy about the mark on her arm, but Sammy had already gone inside. I suspected that she might have gotten the bruise from Shark or perhaps she might have bumped into a wall or something. I didn't even mention my suspicion about Shark to Mom or anybody.

Speaking of Shark, he once again was waiting for Sammy. He just didn't know when to quit with his disturbing surprises. Shark surprised Sammy in the lobby of her building. Sammy ordered Mikey to stay in the entrance for his own safety. She asked Shark what he was doing there.

Shark said, "Why were you hanging with your *retard* boyfriend and his ugly misfit friends?"

It shocked her. Sammy marched up to him and slapped Shark really hard and yelled, "How dare you say such a thing like that! Shorty, Butchie and Stephanie are all my friends and if anybody is an ugly misfit, IT'S YOU!!! NOW LEAVE ME ALONE!!!!!"

Sammy grabbed Mikey's hand very tightly and stormed off. "I told that delusional creep to stay away from Samantha." Shark growled, "It looks like he is going to get it now!"

****

The next day at Blockbuster, I was daydreaming about my time with Sammy last night while I was stocking videos on shelves. I wasn't working as quickly or efficiently as usual.

This caught the eye of my boss, Old Man Edward. "So, Hopkins. You wanna focus on work instead of lollygagging?"

"Sorry, sir." I responded, "I got myself thinking about my date last night."

Old Man Edward interrupted me and asked, "And how was your date, Hopkins?"

I responded, "Well I think…"

Old Man Edward once again interrupted and yelled, "I don't care what you think about your date. What am I, your therapist? Now focus and GET TO WORK!!!!"

I turned and thought to myself, "I have to get a new job." I worked twice as hard until Ernie Anderson entered the door.

"Hey, Shorty." Ernie asked me, "What's the good word?"

I responded, "Hi, Ernie, I went out with Sammy last night."

Ernie asked me, "Oooooo, how was that?"

"Well we had a really good time." I explained to Ernie, "We went out to Smokey Jones Pizza and after dinner, we went to the movies across the street. It was really good. We both agreed that it's the best movie of the year."

"Good for you, Shorty." Ernie responded as he patted me on the shoulder. "I'm happy for you."

****

Meanwhile at Fordham, Sammy had to cover for her Algebra teacher's class while her teacher was in a meeting. Most of the students were sleeping in class, while others like Maureen are listening.

Caitlin didn't come to class because she wasn't feeling well. Afterward, when Sammy and Maureen were leaving class, Maureen asked Sammy about her date last night.

"It wasn't really a date. Well, Shorty seems nice," Sammy responded. "He and his friend Butchie can sing pretty good together."

Maureen asked, "How was the movie?"

Sammy believes the movie was really incredible. "I had a really fun night. The only problem I had is that idiot Shark was waiting for me in the lobby of my apartment building when I got home."

Sammy was concerned about this. "I should have called the cops on that idiot."

"Oh girl, you don't need a cop." Maureen responded. "All you need to do is just hit him with a shovel."

Sammy wants to change the subject. They were talking about renting a movie to watch. The girls were walking towards CVS, where Sammy works, and Blockbuster, where I work.

When they got to my store, Sammy saw me putting videos on shelves. We were surprised and happy to see each other and she introduced me to Maureen. I forgot to tell her that I was going to work today.

I asked nervously, "So to what do I owe the pleasure of your visit?"

Sammy responded, "We're here to rent a video."

I asked them, "What kind of video do you like?"

Sammy responded, "What do you recommend?"

I said, "Well we have chick-flick movies and…"

Maureen interrupted and growled at me, "We don't do chick flicks."

"Sorry," I apologized and explained, "I don't know anything about chick-flicks. I just know some people call them chick-flicks. What's a chick-flick anyway?"

"Oh brother," Maureen said.

I figured it was time to move on and asked, "Well then what would you like to get?"

"A comedy…or a romantic movie," Maureen responded. "Everybody likes a good love story."

"That's a great idea, Maureen," Sammy chimed in.

"I thought a romantic movie IS a chick-flick," I thought to myself. "Isn't that what girls really like? I certainly don't want to be offensive to women, but I always thought that a chick-flick and love story are one and the same. I guess Maureen doesn't like the term 'chick-flick.'"

"Maybe I should ask somebody who can help you, girls." I said as Sammy and Maureen walked away.

As I went back to work, the girls went to my other co-worker, Rasheeda Jones. She found a movie for them.

After I finished stocking videos on shelves, I started walking across the store. I saw Sammy and Maureen leaving. Sammy looked back towards me. She smiled and waved. I waved back as she closed the door.

When I stood there for too long, Old Man Edward yelled, "HOPKINS!!!"

I said, "Gotta go."

As I ran off, Old Man Edward complained to himself, "You just can't get good help these days."

****

The Hamilton Brothers were in the dumpster in the alleyway all night long. A garbage man opened the latch and was surprised to see two young men in the dumpster.

"What are you kids doing in there?" the garbage man asked.

The boys, who smelled really bad, were thrilled that they finally got out.

"Oh thank God," Victor said gratefully to the garbage man. "You're a lifesaver, man."

"Yeah," Billy chimed in as they hugged him. The garbage man was REALLY grossed out. He was glad when they stopped hugging him and took off.

As the Hamilton Brothers ran off, the garbage man started taking the bags out of the dumpster.

Everyone on the sidewalk was stepping away from the guys because they smelled so badly and were going insane from the stench; one actually went back inside and parents were trying to back their children away from them.

"MY EYES!!!!" One guy screamed as he drove past them. The driver's eyes were burning and watering and the car was swinging around disastrously and crashed into a wall.

Victor spotted a young woman and tried to hit on her. "Ugh!" Some lady yelled, "You guys stink!"

"It's not me," Victor said. "It is HIM!"

"Nah-uhh!" Billy responded. "It is HIM who is so stinky!!"

Victor yelled, "Am not!"

Billy responded, "Are too!"

They were arguing and wrestling each other to the ground like piggies until Victor reminded himself and stopped.

"Wait! Wait! Wait! Wait! Wait!" Victor shouted. "I think we were in the dumpster all night!"

"Hmmm," Billy puzzled. "I wonder why we went into the dumpster last night?"

Annoyed, Victor reminded Billy, "Dude, don't you remember? We were thrown into the dumpster and we couldn't open the lid. Some nut-job is stealing Shark's girl from him and we needed to report this to Shark immediately."

"Oh my God," Billy replied. "You're right, Vic." He puffed up his chest. "LET'S DO THIS THING!!!" he said in a superhero tone.

"After we go home and take a shower, we will go find Shark." Victor said.

"I called it first," Billy shouted.

"Oh no you don't!" Victor shouted back as he pushed Billy aside. "I do!"

Enraged, Billy charged towards Victor and pushed him aside. Billy kept running until Victor screamed in agony, yelling that his leg was broken. Billy was going to comfort him until Victor got up and ran off for a shower. Billy realized he was tricked. They kept arguing about who gets to take a shower first. Seriously, those guys are absolutely children.

****

I left Blockbuster and was heading home from work. I softly talked to myself, saying lines from cartoons and seeing images in my head. Sometimes I like to make sure no one hears me. Mom warned me before that not everybody understands autism.

I don't have a mental illness; I just like to entertain myself with my busy brain. Some people think that talking to myself is pretty creepy. But for me, it feels natural and fun. The world would be a boring place if we were all the same.

Suddenly, Shark appeared out of nowhere. "Didn't expect to see you here, Hopkins."

The devious voice frightened me. I recognized him as the guy who attacked me at Blockbuster a few days ago. "H...hey, I remember you from Blockbuster the other day." I nervously smiled. "How are you, uh...?"

"How was your date last night, Hopkins?" Shark asked.

"Date?" I replied nervously. "Oh no, no, no, no, no, no, no, no. It wasn't really a date, Sammy and I were just...getting to know each other. That's all."

"Oh really?" Shark asked evilly.

Once again, he angrily grabbed me by the shirt and shoved me against the wall in an alleyway.

Shark yelled, "KEEP YOUR SCHIZOPHRENIC HANDS OFF OF MY ANGEL!!!" I swallowed in fear. "Let me warn you for absolutely the last time, you delusional freak! The next time you see, talk or think of my Eve, you leave me no choice but to sentence you to hell where you belong under God's order." I was horrified when he said that. "Get the picture, *retard*?"

I nodded while I bent my head down sadly as he put me down. "Good boy." Shark said with a grin.

I bent my head down sadly as he put me down... oh wait, I already said that. Sorry. Shark asked me this sadistic question, "Aaaaawwwww!! What's the matter, Hopkins?" Shark chuckled, "Do you need to go back to the *retard* school?"

I sadly shook my head.

"See ya round, Hopkins!" Shark fat-shamed me. "Get it? Round? Cuz you're round?" It was really offensive that he would say such a thing. I should not be surprised. After all, I know that he is pretty mean and would have the guts to make fun of anybody. Fat, skinny, tall, short or whatever. It's almost like he thinks he's perfect.

As Shark left, I felt like I had been threatened once again.

****

Later that night, Sammy and Maureen were at Sammy's apartment, watching the end of "The Sound of Music." I haven't watched the movie as much, but my Mom and my sister watched it many times and they say it is really good, as good as the movie I saw last night: "Disney's Beauty and the Beast."

I have seen the actress Julie Andrews many times since she was in "Disney's Mary Poppins." I watched that movie many times with my big sister Molly. The girls really enjoyed "The Sound of Music" and chatted about it.

As Sammy went up to go to the bathroom, she saw her grandmother watching TV. There was a program on one of the tallest buildings in the world, the World Trade Center. Of course you all know them better as the Twin Towers. Sammy goes there sometimes to think straight. She had an idea, a pleasant idea. Sammy got a wonderful pleasant idea and said, "I know just what to do!"

****

I got home from work. Mom, who was carrying the groceries with Butchie, asked me how work was today and I responded, "Exhausting."

As I walked to the bathroom I also said, "Uneventful."

Butchie and Mom were both worried about my behavior because I didn't talk much about what had happened at work. Like I said before, as much as I don't like to talk about things, I'm aware that it's not always good to keep things to yourself. I was thinking about talking to them about seeing Sammy at Blockbuster today and how Shark threatened me again.

Suddenly, the phone rang. Mom picked it up. It was Sammy. She asked if Shorty was around.

"He's not available right now," Mom responded.

"Okay," Sammy asks Mom for a favor. "Please ask him to call me back when he has a chance."

"Okay, Sammy." Mom replied.

They hung up as I came out of the bathroom. I wanted to tell Mom the news about Sammy coming to Blockbuster today.

As I did, Mom told me, "Speaking of Sammy, she just called while you were in the bathroom and asked if you could call her back."

I was worried about whether or not I should return Sammy's call. Annoyed by this, Mom made the decision for me. "Just call Sammy back!"

Since I got her number at the meeting, I dialed 212-612-1992. Sammy answered the phone. We said hello to each other. Sammy invited me to go to the World Trade Center the next afternoon. I was confused at first because I'm not good with locations. She explained to me what it is. I figured it was the towers I've seen in the movies.

I responded, "Of course I will go."

Sammy was glad to hear me say that. We said goodbye to each other and hung up. I explained to Mom about Sammy inviting me to go to the Twin Towers with her tomorrow afternoon.

Meanwhile, Sammy reported the news to her grandmother, Joan. Joan was still concerned about her time with me. Mikey once again teased his sister about her "boyfriend." This annoyed her. Sammy headed back to her room with Maureen, who overheard her complain to her grandmother.

She asked Sammy, "What's wrong, girl?"

Sammy responded, "Nothing." Maureen didn't want to make things worse so she hugged her while Sammy was crying. Shark scared her, but her overprotective grandmother bothered her too.

****

Meanwhile, Shark is sitting in his room at the deserted building that he refers to as his "Garden of Eden," reading the Bible. He had moved to the old warehouse after his family "abandoned" him.

Inside the room, there are religious pictures hung up on the walls. Bibles are laid out to read, candles for light and small religious figures are cluttered all about the tiny space. A large crucifix with a bleeding and suffering Jesus is on the wall. Jesus has an expression of total agony and this crucifix is the focal point of the little room. He named the place "The Garden of Eden," the biblical "garden of

God", described in the Book of Genesis chapters 2 and 3, and also in the Book of Ezekiel.

Suddenly, Victor and Billy opened the door. "Shark, you would not believe what we saw…"

An exasperated Shark groaned and responded in a low, menacing tone, "How many times have I told you stupid *retards* not to come barging in like that?!" He slapped each of them in the face really hard with the Bible.

"Sorry, sir," The Hamilton Brothers responded as they backed up from Shark, who was panting heavily. They reported the news to him about seeing Sammy and me together.

Shark became furious to learn that I had been with Sammy against his direct order to not see her. The Hamilton Brothers were horrified by how angry Shark became.

He swore revenge as he growled in his villainous breakdown, "That's it! This isn't the first time that dim-witted thieving worthless piece of garbage bothered my Eve, but I will tell you this: it will be the LAST TIME!!!!"

****

The next day, it was a beautiful sunny day. The sun is shining and the birds are singing. Sammy and I were walking and chatting about our plans for the day at the Twin Towers.

"Well I want to go to the observation deck later," she said. "It's really cool up there. You get to see everything from up there. You can see all of Manhattan."

"Are you sure about this, Sammy?" I was nervous about going there at first.

"Don't approach something negatively." Sammy explained, "It's good to try new things. You can't just do the same thing everyday; otherwise I'll call you BORING!!!!"

"Okay, Sammy." I laughed, "Sounds like you can be a little bossy."

"So why haven't you and your mother ever gone up there?" Sammy asked, "She would probably really enjoy it."

"Are you crazy?" I shouted, "My mother is afraid of heights. She feels sick to her stomach and dizzy if she's up high. She's better off staying on the ground." Sammy laughed.

When we made it to the World Trade Center, one of her favorite places in the world to think, I was really surprised on how tall those buildings are, both on the outside and the inside. They have really cool stuff in these towers. Sammy sure found a really cool place to hang out.

While we were having fun, we ran into a guy with an Irish accent named Paddy Power, who is a good friend of Sammy's. He's a really nice guy.

We went to eat lunch at the Windows of the World restaurant, which is located on the 106th floor of the North Tower. It is really beautiful there. We sat at a table near the full-length windows. I was looking out and it was incredible. I felt like I was floating from that height. I explained to Sammy that when I was a kid, my father always lifted me onto his shoulders and I always imagined myself flying in the sky like a bird or Disney's "Peter Pan."

Sammy responded with a giggle, "That's cute, Shorty."

Suddenly, Angie and Dreggs appeared. "Well, well. Hello there, Johnson."

I waved with a smile and Sammy responded as she sighed, "Oh Jesus. Hello, Angie."

Angie introduced Peter just to insult Sammy; "I would like to introduce you to my boyfriend, Peter Dregg…"

"I know, Angie!" Sammy shouted. "I know!!"

She knows Angie keeps introducing Dreggs just to make her feel bad about her breakup with Shark.

I asked Sammy, "What's wrong, Sammy?"

Angie responded that Sammy is being dramatic and Dreggs giggled. Sammy explained who she is and said that Angie has been insulting her for many years.

I responded, "Well that's not very nice at all."

Dreggs defended Angie, saying that she is just being friendly.

Angie responded as she kissed him on the check, "You really are awesome, Peter."

I responded, "Well I think only a complete moron would fall for that."

Shocked by my "harsh" statement, Dreggs responded, "Excuse me?"

I insulted them with a big speech, "Yeah, you heard me. You're both pathetic. No wonder, your mommies dropped you on your heads when you were babies. And did you really think you could make fun of Sammy just for the fun of it? No. Not you two dopes. You are just a couple of losers who like to insult people you think are less powerful just to feel good about yourselves."

People noticed there was trouble brewing while Angie and Dreggs were both shocked about what I had just said. Angie was crying as she walked out the door and Dreggs was chasing after her. Sammy was really impressed that I stood up to them like that.

"Oh no problem," I responded. "They're just a couple of dorks." Sammy giggled. "Besides, if anybody wants to insult you, they'll have to go through me."

"Aw. Thanks, Shorty." Sammy said. "That really means a lot to me."

We left our table as soon as we finished our lunch. She even taught me how to pay a check. I was shocked by this at first, but Sammy explained, "If you want to have a place of your own, then try to be independent."

Angie and Dreggs came back to finish business with us. Unfortunately for them, we were already gone, much to their dismay.

As Angie and Dreggs were heading back to their table, Angie bumped into a tough girl.

The girl yelled, "Watch where you and your caboose are going!"

Angie was shocked as Dreggs was giggling and everyone else was laughing. She slapped him.

Dreggs was confused why Angie slapped him so hard like that, "What? What did I do?" Dreggs asked as they went back to their FANCY seats.

****

After we left the Windows of the World restaurant, I was asking Sammy if the observation deck is on top of the building we were in.

"No, Shorty," Sammy replied. "The observation deck is on top of the South Tower."

When we got out of the North Tower, we went to the South Tower. I like to imagine that buildings and other things are like humans and I thought that the North Tower was jealous because we were leaving and going to the South Tower. I debated in my own head do I tell Sammy or would she think I'm a kook. I decided not to tell her that the building might be jealous; even I know that's ridiculous.

The South Tower is as big as the other one. I suddenly saw a sign in the lobby and read it:

"TOP OF THE WORLD Observation Deck World Trade Center Open Daily 9:30 A.M. to 9:30 P.M."

Hours later, we finally got up to the top of the South Tower, which is located on the 107th floor. We had more fun in those elevators before we finally got on top.

Do you guys want to know how we got up there? OK. Here we go.

Their elevators have to go higher than any other elevators in the world. At first when I got out of the elevator, I saw the window and mistakenly thought it was the observation deck.

"We're not at the observation deck yet, Shorty." Sammy reminded me, "It's right on top."

"Oh," I replied. "Then how do we get there?"

We rode one of the two short escalators up from the 107th floor to the 110th floor. The sky had a beautiful sunset and the wind was breezy. I was very impressed when we got to the top of the WTC South Tower observation deck as birds were cawing in the distance.

"Oh my G...Holy shoot!" I shouted out in amazement.

"I can see everything from up here. I can see the Statue of Liberty, the river and a lot of buildings that are much smaller than these towers, even the Empire-State Building."

I expressed my opinion about the WTC view, which I got from a movie I saw once.

"It all looks so neatly laid out, so...civilized...from up here, doesn't it?" I asked. "Like there's some kind of logic to it all. It's all so clear. But you get down there on the street and it's all crazy!."

"Wow, Shorty. That was pretty deep." Sammy replied, "Where did you learn that?"

"Sorry. I got it from a movie once," I told her. "You know what I mean?"

Sammy agreed as she asked me, "You know what it's like to view something like this?"

"No," I responded. "What?"

Sammy answered, "It's like you can see the entire world."

"Hey!" I shouted as I looked through the telescope and pointed out, "I can see my apartment from here." My point of view of the observation deck made me compare to the Wonkavator ending scene from "Willy Wonka and the Chocolate Factory." Remember when the boy and his grandfather crashed through the glass ceiling and the elevator was floating and flying, and they could see everything from up in the sky?

Suddenly, Sammy started to become very sad. She was looking at a happy family nearby. An image of her parents flashed through Sammy's mind.

I noticed the look on Sammy's face and asked, "What's wrong, Sammy?"

Sammy responded, "Nothing."

"Come on, Sammy," I said. "You can tell me." She explained her past, her tragic loss to me, "My parents died years ago."

"Oh," I replied. "Sorry to hear that. Did you tell anybody else about it?"

"No, I don't like to talk about it too much." Sammy said in a melancholy way, "It hurts too much."

Sammy is trying her best to hold back tears, but she couldn't because of all the pain she's feeling.

"So what happened to them?" I asked, "If you don't want to talk about it, I understand."

As much as Sammy doesn't like to talk about it, she still trusts me to tell the truth.

Sammy shared with me that she was born in Westerly, Rhode Island on Wednesday, May 20, 1970. She was only 13 years old when Mikey was a baby in 1983.

Their mother sang them to sleep and their father worked as a salesman at a car dealership.

Sadly, their parents died in a plane crash. Sammy and Mikey were sent to live with their grandparents in New York City. Sammy has been trying to deal with her loss ever since. Not only did she lose her parents, but she also lost all her friends in Rhode Island when she had to move to New York.

"Since I moved here," Sammy continued as tears were running down her face, "I have tried to get along with others, but it feels like they always have to hurt me in some way no matter where I go. They call me names, and judge me by who I spend time with. No matter what I do, I can't get away from the insults. You have no idea what it's like to feel like a loser. It's a waste of my time. I'm a waste of time."

This story makes me realize that Sammy has very low self-esteem. Mom taught me the dangers of low self-esteem issues. It's sad though. I started to feel sorry for Sammy when she started crying, weeping tears. Seeing the tears fall from Sammy's eyes, I felt my heart tighten all of a sudden. Maybe it's because I hated to see her in pain like this.

"No, Sammy. Don't say that. You're not a waste of time." I comforted her with a hug and gently patted her back as I said, "It's okay, Sammy. I'm here."

I helped her take a couple of deep breaths and helped her think about her happy place. "Sammy, think about all the wonderful things in your life. When I do that, it helps get rid of all the pain." It cheered her up and I shared my loss of my father with Sammy.

"When I lost my father, my mother explained that heaven is our real home; we're only on this Earth for a little while. We are in heaven for all eternity," I explained. "Besides, your parents are fine in heaven and you have your own guardian angels watching over you. I am sure they're very proud of you and your little brother. You must miss them very much. And finally, no matter what happens, I think you're always a winner in my book."

"You really think so?" Sammy asked.

"Yeah," I replied, "I know so."

Her tears went from sadness to gratitude and thankful as Sammy looked up at me.

She said, "You're so sweet."

After that statement, Sammy and I got back to watching one of the most beautiful views in the whole world.

"Man," I said, "this is a beautiful spot to watch the sunset."

Sammy responded, "Well you know what they say."

I asked, "What?"

Sammy answered, "The perfect end to a perfect day."

I put my hand into hers.

She noticed my hand on hers. "Um, Shorty. You can let go of my hand now."

"Oh sorry." I said as I blushed and let her hand go.

As soon as the sun went down, we decided to go back down and head home.

Well those were pretty interesting and touching moments, huh? To be honest, I always try to help people by consoling them in a very positive way, no matter how traumatic their events and problems can be. I understand not everything is a cartoon, but sometimes, I wish life could be.

The cartoon characters can do things on screen that real life people can't. In real life, people don't get flattened like a pancake and then regain their original form. You guys know what I mean by that. Right? Right?

$$***************************$$

Later that evening after our fun day at the Twin Towers, Sammy and I were walking back home.

"You sure found a great place to hang out, Sammy," I said.

Sammy replied, "Why thank you, Shorty."

We were talking about what was our favorite part of our trip. I mostly like the observation deck and Sammy mostly liked the way I stood up to Angie and Dreggs for her. Sammy admitted that she really enjoyed her time with me.

When we walked by a dark alley, a flipped out Shark appeared out of the shadows and he let out a bloodcurdling roar, "HOPKIIIINNSSSS!!!!"

We were both frozen by his terrible sound. Sammy asked Shark what he was doing here. I realized immediately that it's the same scary guy who threatened me at Blockbuster twice. "Not now, Samantha," he yelled.

He turned to me and coldly asked, "What did I say about hitting on my angel?"

"No, no, please!" I begged. "I can explain."

"I gave you a second chance and THIS IS WHAT I GET?!!" Shark shouted.

"I'm sorry." I begged. "It's just that…"

"Yeah?" Shark barked. "Well here's what you can do with your apology you *RETARD*!!!!"

Shark brutally punched me in the face, much to Sammy's horror. "How does it feel, you worthless piece of *crap*?!!!!" Shark shouted as he leaned down into my face. "No, I'm wrong. You're lower than crap!!!! You're a *RETARD*!!!!"

Shark grabbed her by the wrist and headed towards the alleyway, yelling "MY ANGEL!"

Sammy yelled, "Let go of me!"

"You're supposed to be **my** future Mary, not some fat potato headed *RETARD'S*!!!!" Shark shouted and he quoted **Genesis 3:13** as he shoved her against the wall,

"And the Lord God said unto the woman, What is this that thou hast done? And the woman said, The serpent beguiled me, and I did eat."

When Shark grabbed Sammy's head and kissed her, she punched Shark in the face and kicked him in his you know what, which made Shark fall to the ground. Sammy ran back to me as Shark covered his face in pain. Two police officers were nearby and witnessed the assault.

One officer asked, "You folks alright?"

The other officer went to the alleyway where she found Shark. Sammy replied, "That creep just punched my friend and stuck his tongue down my throat!" They immediately recognized Shark and arrested him.

He was yelling as the officers were putting him in the police car, "Get off of me, you snakes!!"

I was crying from the punch. Sammy gave me some tissues for my bloody nose and comforted me as we walked back home.

Unknown to us, while the police were bringing Shark to the station, Shark asked one of the officers, "Do your kind have the right to do anything?!"

The officers were offended by his racist comments and they threatened him, ordering him to keep quiet.

Shark "apologizes" to the officers, stating, "Well I'm sorry, I was surprised that there are black cops and not just black criminals!!"

The officers ordered him once again to keep his mouth shut.

"Sheesh this guy's a racist!!" One of the officers asked the other, "Where did this guy even come from?"

"Well this guy might just go to hell." the other officer replied.

"Actually,..." Shark said as he freed himself from the handcuffs, grabbed one of their guns, and shot the officers, killing both of them. This caused the car to crash into a fire hydrant, spraying water like rain everywhere, and then the car hit a building. He ran away from the damaged police car.

Shark looked back at the dead police officers and said with a grin, "...I was going to say the same thing about **you.**"

It showed he has no remorse or empathy for what he just did to those poor officers. Shark ran off like the coward he is.

From that point on, Shark became increasingly more fixated on causing harm to me out of a genuine hatred and rage toward me.

****

Back at home; Mom was taking notes while she was talking on the phone. Butchie and Stephanie were sitting on the couch together, watching their favorite comedy movie. They thought it was really funny, but Mom and I always thought that movie was completely insane.

"Oh my God!" Stephanie asked, "Was this the funniest movie ever or what?"

Butchie said, "Well I really enjoyed watching it with you, Babe."

Stephanie smiled and said in a flirtatious tone, "You're the best boyfriend ever, Butchie Camastro."

Butchie responded, "And you're the best girlfriend ever, Babe."

They were kissing until Sammy and I came to the door. I was still in pain from Shark's punch. Mom got off the phone because she was horrified to see my face badly hurt. Mom told her friend, "I better call you back." Sammy explained what happened after we left the Twin Towers.

Mom asked me if that's true and I tearfully nodded. "It was terrible, Mom. He didn't have to punch me."

Mom was so sorry to hear that Shark had punched me and said that I should stay away from people like that. Mom asked Sammy how she came to know that psychopath. Sammy revealed Shark's backstory.

Sammy explained that when she reached high school, she thought Shark was the cutest boy ever. She didn't know he was so dangerous at the time and also 12 years older then she was. Shark hid it very well and always hung out where the high school kids were, like the roller-skating rink and the hamburger place. Sammy felt "invisible" except around her best friend Maureen, Maureen's partner Caitlin, her annoying and shy little brother Mikey, and her overprotective grandmother Joan. Sammy thought if she dated him, she wouldn't be "invisible" anymore. She didn't realize that Shark only cared about her appearance.

Shark seemed nice enough when they first started interacting with one another. However, things changed. Shark turned out to be a big mistake. He psychologically and physically abused her badly. "It's a miracle." Shark once said aloud what he thought to himself. "God chose you to be my angel of salvation." Sammy went through unspeakable torture that Shark inflicted on her. He thought he was in charge of her and was jealous of anyone who came close to her. One time, Shark broke her arm as "punishment" for her "sin." But she didn't sin, Shark is just saying twisted words. He said it was an accident but he grabbed her arm way too hard. Shark bullied, insulted, and controlled her to make sure that he kept her all to himself. He also bullied and verbally abused disabled people, much to her horror. She believed that Shark felt better when he beat up disabled and weaker people. Sammy guessed that he was beaten up as a child. He felt strong and powerful when he beat up others.

One day, Shark saw Sammy hugging her friend Gary, the guy who Ernie was talking about the other day, and beat him up in a fit of jealousy and rage. Shark knew that Gary was gay and he was not trying to steal Sammy from him. Shark hated homosexuals. He believed what it said in **Leviticus 20:13,**

"If a man lies with a man as one lies with a woman, both of them have done what is detestable. They must be put to death."

Frightened, Sammy told him to stop beating up Gary, but he shoved her to the ground and gave her a black eye. Shark never felt bad about it. Sammy always tried to stop him when he wanted to hurt someone, but Shark ignored her, saying she had become hysterical.

When Sammy realized that Shark was cheating on her with his gym trainer, he carelessly brushed it off like nothing happened. Sammy quickly realized her big mistake in ever going out with Shark. When he later explained his whole complicated life to her, Sammy knew he was a very troubled human being While she liked to believe everyone has good qualities, maybe Shark was "TOO FAR GONE."

Shark was born in Kansas on Sunday, April 20, 1958, His late manipulative and cruel father, Jack Roderick Sr. was one of the leaders of the KKK (Ku Klux Klan) and taught him about religion. He told him that people who are different are "God's mistakes" who came from the Devil. Jack Sr. ultimately disagreed with Dr. King's speeches about equality and respect for all people.

Jack Sr. was sent away to prison when Jack was eight years old. He thinks a bunch of devils, which Jack Sr. calls the police officers, carried Jack Sr. away for burning a cross on a black family's front lawn. Jack Sr. blamed his son for his arrest and told everyone that he wishes he could disown him like he never even wanted a child. He eventually died in prison.

Meanwhile, Jack felt betrayed by his father and came to hate him. So Jack began attending a fundamentalist church group. He thought the church might help him get rid of the devil in himself and he really believes he is helping God.

Over the years since Jack moved to New York City, his neglectful mother, Margaret Roderick, got involved in serious relationships with different kinds of men. She was a stripper and a prostitute. Jack was sent to live with his mother after his father went to prison and died. Jack denounced her, believing that she was living in sin.

All of her partners were abusive toward Jack. His mother didn't care. She always acted so cold to him because his father mistreated her. She always thinks of Jack Roderick Sr. when she sees her son and those are not pleasant memories for her.

Meanwhile, Jack was misunderstood, miserable, nerdy, and he was always a scapegoat. He had a long-time interest in religion and thought he always followed his faith. He believed that the world is a dark cruel place and everyone around him was "breaking God's rules." Everyone was laughing at him, including the students at school, his teachers, and his own mother.

When Jack was fourteen, his mother's boyfriend beat him up. Jack finally snapped. He fumed with anger and brutally beat him up. He believed what was said in **Proverbs 22:24-25**

"Make no friendship with a man given to anger, nor go with a wrathful man, lest you learn his ways and entangle yourself in a snare."

The boyfriend ended up in the hospital and his mother disowned Jack as she bellowed, "You listen to me you worthless piece of *crap*! No matter what you do for the rest of your life, you'll always be garbage! I'm embarrassed to call you my son."

She turned her back on her own son. Upset, sad, forgotten, heartbroken, shocked, devastated, unhappy and frustrated, Jack now believes that his mother doesn't care about him anymore and sees her as bad as his father.

Once again, Jack snapped. He was starting to believe that all love is just a myth since he never got any affection from his parents. His mother only ignored him and his father physically and mentally abused him. He refuses to forgive them for the pain, suffering and agony they gave him. His mother eventually died of a heart attack from frustration and rage. Jack never admitted to feeling sad about his mother dying.

Jack found an empty house and made it into his own "church" and named it the "Garden of Eden." He planned on living there and getting more people who thought like he did to come to church there. He only wanted "perfect" people in his church. He believed what was said in **Leviticus 21:17-18:**

"None of your descendants, throughout their generations, who has any blemish shall come forward to offer the food of his God. Anyone who has any of the following blemishes may not come forward: he who is blind, or lame, or who has a split lip, or a limb too long, or a broken leg or arm."

Jack believed that he was fixing the "mistakes" God made. Jack was clearly delusional. He started calling himself Shark at this time because he thought he was a predator to "God's mistakes." He actually tried to kill a neighbor's dog by throwing rocks at it. He was hoping the neighbor, who had an intellectually disabled child, would move away from the neighborhood if the dog died. The dog lived, but Shark's cruelty became known to everyone nearby.

Shark explained to Sammy that he had a deep desire to kill anyone who got in his way. He was filled with so much hatred and prejudice. Disturbed when Sammy learned all about Shark's past, she immediately made an excuse to leave. When she got home, she called and broke up with him.

"How could you be so selfish, so cruel?" She asked. "How could I have been so blind?"

"When the time comes," Shark warned her, "You will know your place."

"I've never been treated that way in my whole life," Sammy cried. "I never wanted to see you again, you miserable MONSTER!!!"

Shark became over-obsessed with getting Sammy back and has been stalking her ever since. When will he ever leave her alone?

Mom listened carefully to Sammy's tale and said, "That's horrible."

Sammy and I explained about the police arresting Shark for assaulting us.

Mom said, "Well at least he will be punished now and can't bother you two anymore."

As Sammy was about to leave, I thanked her for the nice day we had together before things went crazy with Shark. She smiled and left.

"Ooooooo Shorty!" Stephanie excitedly stated, "I think she likes you!"

I reminded her that we're just friends and Mom said, "That was quite a story Sammy shared with us. No wonder she is training to be a therapist after knowing a guy like that."

"What a jerk that Shark is," I responded. "Sammy and I had such a nice day before we saw him. That place was incredible. It has everything in it. Sammy and I ran into a good friend of hers. I don't remember what his name is, but he's a really nice guy and we had lunch at this restaurant called uhhh…"

Mom figured out what I was talking about.

Mom answered, "Windows on the World?"

"Yes!" I shouted out, "That's right, Windows on the World! Thank you, Mom."

"Sheesh!" Mom said, "Lower your volume, Shorty!"

"It was really cool when we went to the top." I continued, "It has an amazing view."

Mom said, "Well I'm glad you guys had fun."

"Me too, Mom," I responded. "Me too."

When I said that, I felt like I was involved in a classic show.

****

Officer John Wall and his partner Detective Paul "Paulie" Martino were both assigned to the case of Sergeant Louis Adams and Officer Patricia Riker's murders. They set out for an investigation.

After arriving at the crime scene, they were shocked when they saw a damaged police car crashed into a wall and a fire hydrant, spraying water like rain everywhere. There are unclear sounds from the radio chatters. The paramedics were carrying the bodies on the stretchers. They passed the "do not cross" line.

Officer John spoke to one of the witnesses, Old Man Edward. "Alright, sir. We're gonna ask you a question. I want to know what you've seen so far, understand?"

Old Man Edward arrogantly responded, "Whatever you say, Officer!"

Detective Martino asked, "Who killed them?"

"Well I have no idea!!" Old Man Edward responded, "I don't know who he is and didn't even see his face! All I know is that he had a black leather jacket! I'm sure that ladies love him!"

Officer John tried to convince him that this is not a joke, but Old Man Edward rudely interrupted John and Paulie. "Besides, if I were you guys, I would waste my time eating donuts for the rest of my life! I feel like I couldn't do anything about it when this happened! So what do you say to that, Bozos?!"

Old Man Edward was laughing at the insult, which angered Officer John. He shouted as he charged at Old Man Edward while Paulie held him back. "Who are you calling a Bozo, you son of a…?"

"Relax, John." Paulie convinced John, "He's just messing with us."

Annoyed by Old Man Edward's obnoxious behavior, they move on to someone else as Old Man Edward shouts, "So you call yourself a police officer! Heh heh heh heh! You can't catch me. Maybe you should catch a cold! You know what I'm going to do to you? I should pop you right in the nose!"

Old Man Edward was charging at Officer John as he yelled. Unfortunately for him, he accidentally hit his face into a pole and he fell to the ground, unconscious.

The police captain, who happens to be Caitlin's father, John Oliver, called out for John and Paulie. He explained to them who the perpetrator is as he gave them Shark's criminal record files.

As they were reading the files, Captain Oliver explained, "Hunting down Shark is my number one priority, even if it means I die trying."

"Don't worry, sir," John replied, "We'll be happy to take him down."

"This guy is some kinda Jesus freak?" Paulie asked.

"Yes," Captain Oliver explained. "His ex-girlfriend was trying to warn everyone about what a monster he is. But unfortunately, there were not enough charges against him."

"Well that sounds serious," John replied.

Captain Oliver also warned them that he hopes they were trained very well. "You guys got yer work cut out for you," he said. "Because you're about to hunt one of the most dangerous outlaws in this city."

****

Victor and Billy were at Shark's place when they heard the news on TV about Shark's arrest. They were thrilled to hear he had been caught and arrested because they were afraid of him. The Hamilton Brothers put a tape in the cassette player and played their favorite song as a celebration.

They did not hear the news report about the dead policemen or Shark's escape because they were too busy celebrating Shark's arrest. Victor was lead singer and Billy was the background singer. Sometimes they sing together. It's pretty entertaining, catchy, and funny.

"The Hamilton Brothers"

Victor: Shark is the devil.

Billy: Got that right.

Victor: We are free men.

Billy: I'm with you, Brother.

Victor: Nobody can tell us what to do anymore.

Billy: Why?

Victor: Because we're The Hamilton Brothers.

Billy: Yeah!!!!

Together: We've always been losers all our lives.

But now it's our lucky day.

Chicks will love us.

Because we're the Hamilton Brothers! That's who we are.

Victor: You can't tell us what to do.

Billy: Yeah!!!!

Victor: Shark, we're through with you.

Billy: Got that right.

Victor: You can't tell us what to do.

Billy: Yeah...what?

Victor: Shark, we're through with you.

Billy: Hm. Déjà vu.

Together: We've always been losers all our lives.

But now it's our lucky day.

Chicks will love us.

Because we're the Hamilton Brothers! That's who we are.

Victor: We're the Hamilton Brothers!

Billy: I'm with you, Brother.

Victor: We were born in the dumpster and a lot of bad things have been happening to us.

Billy: That part I get.

Victor: I hope Mommy is hearing this.

Billy: Hey, Mommy!!!

Victor: How's it feel to be a loser, like Billy?

Billy: Yeah...Hey!!!

Together: We've always been losers all our lives.

But now it's our lucky day.

Chicks will love us.

Because we're the Hamilton Brothers! That's who we are.

YEAH!!!!

They sang and danced like buffoons until the enraged Shark angrily opened the door. It got their attention and they turned off the radio and nervously smiled.

"H...Hi, Sh...Shark!" Victor shuttered. "H...How are you doing, buddy?!"

"Y...Yeah," Billy replied. "W...We heard about what happened to ya on the news. W...We thought the cops had you. A...A...Are you alright...?"

Shark rudely cut Billy off, "Shut up! Hopkins separated me from my angel and turned those pigs on me! Nobody does that to me! EVER!!!! One of these days, that *retard* is going to pay! Oh I'll get him back and he'll be sorry!"

Victor and Billy were both uncomfortable and scared about this as Shark pulled out a gun from his jacket, which he stole from the officers he killed.

They said to each other, "Uh-Oh!"

Shark ordered the Hamilton Brothers to spy on Sammy and me and if they see anything "wrong", they have to report back to him.

"S...S...Sure," Victor shuttered. "but w...w...what about you, man?"

"Oh don't worry, boys," Shark explained evilly. "The rest is up to me."

****

The next morning, Sammy was having a traumatic nightmare about Shark until her alarm clock beeped at 5:30 in the morning. While she was glad she woke up from the nightmare, the alarm going off so early was a little annoying.

She started her day by jogging and studying French like she usually does. Sammy was wearing spandex exercise clothes and her hair was in a ponytail. She feels better when she exercises.

While she was stretching, Shark was stalking Sammy by secretly hiding behind a tree. He was staring at her in a very creepy way. Mom warned me about that kind of stuff. She said that's not what a gentleman does.

After jogging, Sammy went home to take a shower, and get ready for her time with me. When she was about to leave, her grandmother asked Sammy to walk Mikey to school, because she has a busy schedule. While she was walking Mikey to school, Shark continued to spy on her. Sammy thought she heard something. Shark was hiding behind the tree. Sammy thought she was imagining things. Shark was gleefully spying on her. "You truly are an angel." He went to a phone booth and called the boys to make sure they would continue spying on Sammy and me.

****

Meanwhile, the Hamilton Brothers are in their apartment bedroom. They are trying to come up with a plan on how to spy on Sammy and me, as well as trying to help Shark get his revenge. Victor was doing most of the planning because Billy was too tired to come up with a plan. Victor was really annoyed that Billy wasn't focusing on what they needed to do.

Suddenly, their phone rang. The boys childishly fought over who was going to answer the phone. Victor got the phone, much to Billy's dismay.

Victor asked, "HELLLLLOOOOO??!!!!" It was Shark on the phone.

"IT'S ME, YOU NUMBSKULLS!!!!" Shark yelled.

"Sorry, man," Victor replied. "We were just trying to greet you."

"NEVER MIND THAT!!!!" Shark shouted. "Have you found out a way to get rid of Hopkins yet?"

"Well we…" Victor tried to explain.

"SHUT UP!!!!" Shark shouted.

"Yes sir." Victor and Billy said together.

"Now you listen closely, boys." Shark said softly, "Hopkins took my angel from me and he's going to pay for that. You two fools have orders to help me, Jack Nicholas Roderick Jr., with my God-given plan to make Samantha mine forever. Do either of you have any questions?" Shark asked in his evil tone.

The Hamilton Brothers stared at each other for a second and Billy asked, "Yeah, just one. When will you reveal this "God-given plan" to us?"

"You both will learn soon enough." Shark replied softly.

The boys were curious about what Shark was saying. Each of them tried to speak, but Shark rudely interrupted them.

"Now," Shark said coldly. "Good day."

Shark hung up.

"Sheesh," Victor said as he hung up the phone, "I wonder what's his God-given plan?"

"Who knows?!!!" Billy replied. "Maybe it might have something to do with our stink bomb."

"The what?" Victor asked surprisingly.

Billy explained that he had ordered a stink bomb and he was trying to figure out what exactly they will do with it once it arrives.

"We should set up this stink bomb to go off as Hopkins enters his bedroom," Billy said, "That way, Sammy would never want to go near him again."

"Gee, Billy," Victor said. "You actually came up with a good plan for a change."

"What plan?" Billy asked.

"And it's over." Victor sighed.

Just then, there was a knock on the door. Billy thought it was the doorbell.

"That wasn't a doorbell, you idiot!" Victor shouted. "THAT WAS A KNOCK!!!"

The boys once again childishly fought over who would answer the door. Billy opened the door and the mailman handed him a package. After the mailman left, they ran back to their bedroom. Despite Victor's big warning, Billy opened it with a baseball bat, setting off the stink bomb. "Billy, NO!!" The bomb exploded like in a cartoon. The boys were both blown up and completely covered in green slime from the blast.

"You DOPE!!!!" Victor shouted. "What are we going to use to humiliate Hopkins NOW?!!!!"

"Uh, I don't know," Billy replied as he nervously smiled. "But look on the bright side, at least it works, right?" Victor was about to beat up Billy.

Their mother came in and called them for breakfast. She shouted, "Why does this place smell so bad?!"

Victor said, "Billy thought it was a good idea to open a stink bomb package with a baseball bat!"

Billy shouted, "TRAITOR!!!"

"I don't know why you two bozos had a stink bomb delivered, nor do I care." Their mother said, "Just open the windows and clean up the mess right now."

In response to the request, Victor started to back-talk his mom by telling her "to do what all good mothers do and get cleaning." Then he left the room with Billy. "And make it snappy!"

Billy asked, "Why would you talk to our mother like that, Vic?"

"Because like what Shark said, Billy," Victor explains. "Mothers are always annoying, Pea brain."

"Oooooohhhhh!!!!" Billy responded. "Now I get ya, man."

Their mother punished the boys by hitting them with a newspaper and then she forced them to clean up the mess they had made while she went out to go grocery shopping.

Sometime after the Hamilton Brothers finished cleaning up the mess, Victor spotted something in the grocery bag and he hatched a devious idea to get even with Billy.

"Oh, Billy. Wanna try some..." Victor said evilly as he shook the bag and pulled out the food the boys feared the most: "broccoli?"

"No!" Billy cried. "Not the broccoli!" Both brothers hated broccoli; they had since they were kids.

"C'mon, Billy." Victor said as he chased Billy, "Just a little bite."

"Stay away, green puffy stalky thing!" Billy shouted in fear as he tore out of the room by smashing through the door and "running for his life."

"Eat it, Billy!" Victor said in hot pursuit as he continued to chase Billy.

"You boys are in a world of trouble!" shouted their mother Sharon when she went through the broken door.

****

At my apartment, Mom was watching the news while she was getting herself prepared to go to yoga with Diane. She was shocked when they reported on the news that Shark killed those two police officers and got away.

At the police station, Captain Oliver held a press conference on TV about the murder of Sergeant Louis Adams and Officer Patricia Riker. "I'm issuing an arrest warrant for a psychopathic murderer known as Shark Roderick!"

A knock was heard on the door. Cinnamon was barking out of excitement, much to Mom's chagrin. It was Sammy. Sammy said, "Morning, Betty!"

"Hi, Sammy," Mom asked, "How are you doing?"

"Fine." Sammy replied, "I've been running a few laps this morning. It was kinda therapeutic."

"Well you know what they say," Mom jokes. "It's a major pain in the *ass*." Sammy chuckled.

Mom was about to explain what she just saw on the news until I came out of my room, tired. "Morning!" I said yawning.

"Shorty!" Mom sarcastically said, "You're alive."

I replied as I walked like Frankenstein, "Of course I'm alive."

Mom explained that she and Diane were heading to yoga. "Before I go, I need to tell you kids some bad news." She told them that she heard on TV that Shark killed two police officers and he had gotten away. He had not yet been captured. Sammy and I were stunned.

In order to change the subject because I don't like to talk about anything too dramatic or tragic, I interrupted the conversation between Mom and Sammy. Mom didn't like that. She reminded me, "Shorty, you could have just said "Excuse Me!" I explained that I wanted to talk about something else that wasn't so negative. I quickly told Sammy that my parents went to Washington to support the March on Washington in 1963. Just talking about the March on Washington made my Mom burst into tears of joy. The famous Dr. Martin Luther King Jr's greatest speech made her very emotional.

Mom said to Sammy, "I taught him everything he knows."

I just want to help Sammy understand that Shark is wrong about people who are different. We're all perfect no matter what.

Sammy asked, "Did you and Russell have a chance to talk to Dr. King?"

Mom replied, "Yes, we shook his hand and congratulated him."

She also asked Mom, "Was he a nice man?"

Mom said, "Yes he was. And a great man."

She then turned towards me, "Shorty, I know you don't like talking about tragic things, but you can't always change the subject. Some things just don't disappear. There is a murderer on the loose who is out to get you. I think it would be a good idea to discuss Shark a little bit and figure out how we are going to keep you and Sammy safe."

"Don't worry, Mom," I replied. "I'm not afraid of anything. Not here, no how! Now if you both excuse me, some of us have to get some bbbbrrrrrrrreakfast!"

As I entered the kitchen, Mom whispered, "I don't know what I'm going to do with him right now."

"Well you know what they say, Betty," Sammy replied. "If there's not one thing with that guy, there's another."

Since Sammy missed her breakfast, I asked her if she would like a bowl of my cereal, the one I usually ate almost every single day.

Sammy reminded me, "Well, we all gotta watch our figure." Mom left to go to her yoga class with Diane. She gave Sammy the "what to do" list: Breakfast, cleaning room, Teammates for lunch, watching TV and writing a song. The problem is that Mom doesn't leave the apartment with everything she needs. She always keeps coming in which drives me insane. Where are her keys? Where is her wallet? Where are her gloves? Can she remember anything?" Apparently, I do the same thing, going back and forth to my room. Sometimes, I feel like she gets to do that, but I don't. I feel like we're both a little bit alike.

As we were eating breakfast, Sammy asked me, "So, Shorty. How are you this morning after our little episode yesterday?"

I responded drowsily, "Fine." I asked her the same thing. "What about you?"

Sammy responded, "Oh I don't know. I feel like after what happened last night, I don't think it's safe to be near me. Can you believe he actually killed two police officers? He is really out of his mind."

"It's going to be alright, Sammy," I said to her. "I promise."

"I sure hope you're right, Shorty," Sammy replied. "This whole thing makes me nervous."

"By the way, it was amazing, Sammy." I continued. "The way you were beating up that dork."

Sammy replied, "Well what do you expect me to do?"

I chuckled, "Right on."

When I finished my breakfast. Sammy asked me if we could clean my room.

"Oh umm... No," I shrugged.

Sammy tried to reason with me, saying that if I'm going to be a grown up and live on my own someday, I have to learn how to clean up my mess. There are things in my room that aren't worth saving. I felt nervous about Sammy coming into my room at first.

Sammy asked me, "Do you trust me?"

I responded, "Yeah of course."

Sammy stated, "Then let's get started. Come on."

I opened the door as I said nervously, "I can't believe I'm saying this, but welcome to my room, Sammy!"

She entered my room. Without a trace of disgust, although she said, "God that smell."

I apologized to her for the mess. At least she is not too freaked out like my mother. Sammy promised me she wouldn't touch my stuff, but would help me figure it out. I gave her a tour of my room and what's worth saving. She found it pretty creepy the way I save things that aren't worth saving, like food wrappers, tiny pieces of paper plates and cups.

She gave me a trash bag to put my junk in, so we could put the garbage into a dumpster. I felt like I was part of a cleaning crew.

Sammy was singing the song from the movie until I cut her off by saying, "I get it, Sammy. I get it. Too bad I don't have any forest animals to help us." I still like the song, but I just want to concentrate on what I'm doing. Every time I mention a character or a song, people, including my sister chime in by quoting the character or sing along and they indirectly make me lose my focus on what I wanted to say or what I'm doing. Apparently, some people get insulted when I ask them to stop distracting me. They think I don't like them anymore.

Sammy chuckled. I explained other things that I make connection themes between fantasy and reality. She spotted my Beatles poster. "You're a Beatles fan, huh?"

"Oh yeah." I responded. "In fact I met John Lennon once."

Sammy was amazed, "Get out of here, really?"

"Yeah," I responded. "Years ago, when I was 10 years old. It was 1976. My father took me to Central Park. We played baseball together. When I hit the ball, it went really far. I was searching for it. Suddenly, a nice man with a baby carriage found it. It was John Lennon."

"You dropped this, young fella." John said.

As Lennon handed me back the ball, I said. "You sound funny."

"Oh no," John replied, a smile crossing his face, "I think YOU sound funny."

Offended, I shouted, "DAD!!! This man thinks my voice sounds weird."

"Who thinks your voice sounds weird…" Dad said, as he was shocked to see the iconic rock star.

"In that case," John said, "Good day, gentlemen."

As Lennon left, my father taught me a lot about him. He was one of the Beatles, the most popular rock band in the entire world. I became a big fan ever since that day."

Sammy replied, "That's amazing, Shorty. I'm jealous."

I laughed, "You're starting to sound like my sister."

"Really?" Sammy replied. "Why would she be jealous?"

"Well every time something amazing happens to me," I explained. "She always gets jealous of me."

"I guess she's just trying to be funny," Sammy replied.

I even found my old guitar that was hiding in the closet. Sammy explained that if you clean up the mess, you easily find something that was missing.

I finished filling up the trash bag. Sammy wanted me to show her the things that aren't worth saving and I did. She was so proud of me that I was able to throw away some things. I was smiling and very proud of myself. Sammy has such a way with words.

****

Meanwhile, Mom told Diane what happened to Sammy and me last night while they were walking back to the apartment. Mom was really worried about me getting hurt by a homicidal maniac.

"I don't even know what to do about this, Diane." Mom explained, "There's a psychopath who wants to kill my son."

"Oh my God. That's awful." Diane responded, "Maybe you guys should move."

Mom explained that I would be freaked out by the idea of moving, even more than by what happened. "This has got to be the most complicated thing that's happened since Russell died. I feel like

I'm losing my mind with worry, just like I felt then. I'm so worried about Shorty and he doesn't even grasp how serious this is. After all the tragedy that has happened in our family, I..."

Before Mom could continue the discussion, the women were surprised to see us taking out the trash. "God, you're quite the savior, Sammy."

"Ha! Ha!" I laughed sarcastically, "Very funny, Mom!" Sammy responded with a smirk.

"Shorty let me enter his room and he took out a few of the pieces of junk that are not worth saving."

Mom was impressed as she gave me a high five. "Good work, Shorty."

As we left, Diane asked sarcastically, "Who is this guy and what have they done with Shorty?"

"I don't know," Mom responded. "But I like it!"

****

The Hamilton Brothers were causing chaos. Victor was chasing Billy to make him eat broccoli, which they both utterly despise.

Eventually though, Victor caught Billy and threatened him, "Gotcha! Prepare to scarf…"

Billy smacks Victor's hand with a baseball bat he found nearby. This sends the broccoli flying backwards. "YOWCH!" Victor admits that the hit was painful, "That hurt, Billy."

Billy apologizes and tosses the bat away, over his shoulder, "Gee Vic, I'm sorry."

The broccoli lands in Billy's hand. He now has the upper hand. It is filled with broccoli that he plans to make Victor eat.

Billy shouted, "Ah ha!"

Victor screams, "AAAH!"

Billy shouted as he chased Victor, "Devour the broccoli, Victor!"

Victor replied, "Quit it, Billy!"

The weirdest thing is that Billy was chasing Victor around a tree. Victor secretly got out of the chase while Billy continued to run around the tree, thinking that he is still chasing Victor. Victor decided to watch Billy running around laughing happily.

"Hurry, Billy, you almost got me!" Victor shouted.

"Almost got you, Vic!" Billy replied.

Before they cause chaos again, Victor saw Sammy and me exit the apartment building. It's the same building they live in. He realized that Billy is still running around the tree and he was laughing.

"Hey," Victor said. "It's Hopkins. What's he doing here?"

"I don't know, but..." Billy replied.

"Ssssshhhhhh!!!!" Victor interrupted. "I just got a plan. Come on." They ran off quietly.

They were surprised to realize they live in the same apartment as I do.

As I put my trash into the garbage can, Sammy said, as she patted me on the back, "I'm very proud of you Shorty. You were able to throw away quite a bit of garbage from your room." Sammy said, "Maybe we can go to the Teammates later since you did such a good job."

"Thanks Sammy, and I guess I better can it while I'm ahead." I responded as I chuckled, "Get it, Sammy? Huh? Huh?"

Sammy was confused and said, "Uh, not really, Shorty, but whatever you say!" We headed back to the apartment.

****

Meanwhile, outside near my apartment building, the Hamilton Brothers realized that I'm their neighbor. They had disguised themselves as women in order to make me forget about Sammy. Victor looks ridiculous and Billy looks even more ridiculous.

"So how do I look, Vic?" Billy asked.

"Like an idiot?" Victor belligerently replied. "So you ready to do this?"

"I don't know, Dude." Billy replied as he checks on his skirt. "Maybe this skirt makes me look fat."

"You moron!" Victor shouted. "Didn't you hear what I said? We're just doing this so that way we'll make Hopkins forget about Shark's girl and that way Shark and his girl will probably live happily ever after or whatever. End of story."

"Oooohhhh!!!!" Billy said. "Cool."

Unfortunately for them, a bunch of guys were attracted by their "beauty" and were hitting on them.

"S'up, Babes. How about a kiss?"

The Hamilton Brothers tried to brush them off and get away, but the guys chased after them.

"Hey where are you going, Babes, come on!"

The Hamilton Brothers were running for their lives, screaming like little girls they are. Get it? Because they're dressed up as women. Just so you know, my faithful readers, I'm not making fun of women; I'm just making a joke about the Hamilton Brothers. Are they clowns or what?

****

After we finished dumping my garbage, we went back to my apartment. We talked about what else are we were going to do and we decided to invite Butchie and Stephanie to join us for lunch at the Teammates. Mom reminded me that Butchie was working at Fordham and he probably couldn't take that much time for lunch.

I told my mother that it wouldn't hurt to try to reach them. Sammy agreed. I called the Fordham cafeteria and asked for Butchie. I asked him if he and Stephanie could join us and he said it was a good day for them to go because the cafeteria was closing early and they had no other plans.

"See Mom, it doesn't hurt to try." I teased her like I'm rubbing it in her face.

"Shorty, you don't need to be a wise guy." Mom replied.

Before Sammy and I leave for the Teammates, Mom wanted me to leave my bedroom door open because it airs out the room. I wanted to explain to her why I always leave my door closed, but she doesn't care what I have to say and she's getting tired of me thinking I'm in charge. I was concerned that Cinnamon would mess up my room. Mom explained she'll take her out for a walk while Sammy and I are at the Teammates. Sammy reasons with me that I should be worried about what I'm doing, not what Mom is doing. Mom always gets really annoyed with me asking her what she will be doing while I'm outside of our apartment. I did leave the door open, although it still concerned me. We all left the apartment together.

After Sammy and I said goodbye to Mom and Cinnamon, we went our separate ways. Mom is still concerned about me getting hurt by Shark.

****

Butchie got out of work at the Fordham Cafeteria early. He went to the gym where Stephanie was doing a spin class. She was very hot and sweaty, but said she would love to have lunch at the Teammates.

"Butchie!" Stephanie said, as she was surprised to see him.

Butchie responded, "S'up, Babe."

Stephanie asked, "What are you doing here?"

Butchie explained, "I got off work early today and I was hoping you could go to the Teammates with me. Sammy and Shorty want us to meet them there."

"Oh, Butchie," Stephanie responded, "You're the best boyfriend ever. Let me just take a quick shower and we can go."

Stephanie was quick, like she promised, and she and Butchie walked to the Teammates holding hands. As Stephanie was explaining her day to Butchie, they came across an older woman on her hands and knees, straining to look under shrubs and bushes in the garden.

"Ma'am," Stephanie said, "are you OK? Can we help you with something?"

"Well, no, thank you," she responded. "See, I took my pet gerbil out for a walk, and he ran away."

"Well, that's not a problem you come across every day!" Butchie exclaimed. "But I can help you look." He reached down and took her by the arm to help her up.

"GET YER HANDS OFF A ME!" she roared, smacking at his hands. "OFF!"

"Okay, lady," Butchie responded, "you need to relax!" He let go of her. "Come on, Babe," he said, turning to Stephanie, "Let's go!"

"No, Butchie," she answered. "The lady needs help. Let's give her help."

Butchie really did not want to help the woman because she was not at all thankful for the help, and because he did not like gerbils. But Stephanie was looking at him with a disappointed glare, so he waded into the bushes looking for the gerbil. Butchie got a scratch from the bushes. In a short time, he felt a sharp pinch on his lower leg, and looked down to the gerbil moving away after having bit him. His leg was bleeding.

"Son of a...the thing bit me!" Butchie yelled. "That hurt."

"Butchie sweetheart, are you alright?" Stephanie asked as she comforted him and picked him up.

"You let him get away?" the woman yelled. "Some help you are!"

Butchie was amazed...and a little angry. "That's the thanks I get lady?" he shot back. "C'mon, Babe. It's lunchtime. I've given enough help for one day!" He took her by the hand, and limped off.

But the surly old woman was not done. "Go on," she called out as the two walked away. "Who needs you? And you call that help?"

They headed towards the Teammates holding hands, even though Butchie is still in pain from the bite.

****

Meanwhile, Sammy and I were sitting at the Teammates, talking about some stuff. She had never been there before. I replied, "Well there's always a first time. Butchie and I met Mel Blanc here one time, you know. He was the famous voice actor from the Looney Tunes."

Sammy asked, "You guys sure have had a lot of adventures, haven't you?"

"Yeah," I responded. "We sure are lucky!"

Daphne the waitress showed up and said, "Hello, Shorty."

As I was about to respond, Daphne asked, "What's my name, Shorty?"

When I responded "Daphne," she smiled and gave me a high five.

"You are correct, sir!" Daphne replied. "Is this your girlfriend, Shorty?"

Sammy and I laughed and shook our heads. "No." I introduced Daphne to Sammy. "She's my new independent living helper." I explain. "Sammy here is going to help me learn the things I need to know to leave on my own."

"Have you both decided what to eat or drink?" Daphne asked, "But I know what you're going to have, Shorty." I hysterically laughed in response. Sammy ordered a burger.

"I'll have a hamburger please." Sammy replied.

As Daphne left, Sammy asked me, "You're a connoisseur on chicken fingers and French fries, aren't you, Shorty?"

I asked in response, "What's a connoisseur?"

Sammy explained, "It's an expert on things, like you are with chicken."

"Yeah. I'm part-vegetarian and part meat person." I replied. "It's my body and it's my right to choose."

Sammy replied, "I know, but I'm just trying to help you try out new things." I think she thinks that I should eat healthier food.

Suddenly, an idea popped into my head. I explained that I could use vegetables for an appetizer. Sammy liked the idea and said I should ask Daphne when she came back to our table.

I asked her, "Is it okay for me to have some carrots for an appetizer?"

"Sure, Shorty." Daphne replied, "One fresh carrot coming up!!"

As Daphne left, Sammy was asking about my father since I shared my loss with her when we were on top of the observation deck at the World Trade Center.

"Well my father was one of the best people I have ever known. I shared secrets with him and he was a very smart man. Sometimes I felt neglected every time he watched the news or a sitcom. His greatest passions were baseball (he loved to talk about the finer points of the game), classic movies, music ('60's and '70's much preferred) and his family."

Sammy stated, "Sounds like he was a great guy."

I said, "Yeah, he was."

Sammy asked, "What happened to him?"

As much as I don't like talking about it, I don't want to hold anything back from her.

"Well my father had stage 4 cancer, which was discovered after he was diagnosed with diabetes. My parents warned me about too much sugar. He didn't go to the doctor for years. The doctor said he had 3 years to live in 1982. My mother tried to help him. Sadly it was too late. My last conversation with my father was how funny Mel Blanc was. I wasn't there with him when he died and I'm not proud of it. 1985 was a tough year for me."

"Oh my God, Shorty." Sammy replied.

"And that's not all," I continued. "I also lost a good friend of mine named, George Francis, the same year in a tragic accident. I don't know why it happened." I apparently remember what his prayer card said: "He was kind, caring, had a loving heart and a radiant smile."

"Really?" Sammy asked.

"Yep!" I replied. "Growing up, George was always an energetic child who lit up the room. He loved sports and was a relentless competitor. Whether at a concert or in his car, music was also a huge part of his life. He was one of the best people I have ever known and a cool person to talk to. He was also my sister's best friend's brother. He was like a little brother I never had. I used to visit him every Monday afternoon. We played basketball, we went to the movies, watched cartoons and even listened to the Beatles together. George was remembered as a magnetic personality and he was really generous."

"Wow" Sammy replied. "What happened to him?"

"I know it's crazy." I explained. "He was killed in an accident."

"After he died, his family moved because they didn't feel safe in New York City anymore. When someone dies, it's like losing a favorite toy and never finding it again."

Sammy comforted me and reminded me as she placed her hand on top of my hand, "I'm so sorry, Shorty, It's worse than losing a toy. But like you said yesterday, we're in heaven for all eternity and we're only on this Earth for a short while."

I smiled at her. "Thanks, Sammy."

Suddenly, Butchie and Stephanie came into the Teammates. Butchie was limping noticeably.

"Oh my God!" I said, "What happened to you, man?"

Butchie responded, "I got my ass kicked by an old lady and her gerbil."

"What?" I bellowed. "Why would she do that?"

"I don't know!" Butchie replied. "She's just a crazy old lady."

"Well whoever she was," I stated, "she's gone now."

Butchie answered, "Yeah!"

Butchie and Stephanie sat down at our table. Suddenly, Ace and Gloria showed up to greet us.

"Well, the gang's all here." said Ace.

"Hey guys!" said Gloria. "Oh my God, Butchie. What happened to your face?"

"We were trying to help this old lady and her gerbil, but she smacked my Butchie for no reason, and then the gerbil bit him," Stephanie explained.

"Oh my God, that's awful." Gloria said.

"I probably got rabies from that psycho-rat," Butchie chimed in.

"Oh you don't have to worry about that, son." Ace explained. "What matters is that you two tried to help."

"Thanks, Ace." Butchie replied.

"Oh who's this, Shorty?" Ace asked as he spotted Sammy.

I replied, "Ace, Gloria, this is my good friend, Sammy."

Sammy waved, "Hello."

Gloria said, "Oh you look beautiful."

Sammy replied, "Thank you."

Ace explained, "Shorty told us about you the other night."

Sammy replied, "Not too much, I hope."

Gloria said, "We gotta go. Ace and I need to get back to work. It's good to meet you, Sammy."

Ace said as they left. "Bye, guys."

After Ace and Gloria left, Daphne came over and they both ordered cheeseburgers with French fries. I wanted to talk about cartoons and movies, but Sammy wanted to talk about how the old lady and gerbil thing happened earlier. Butchie and Stephanie both explained everything. I reminded them about the psycho that insulted Sammy and me last night.

Sammy glared at me, "Shorty!"

I responded, "Sorry."

Apparently, Sammy did not want me to talk about last night because she had a harsh tone in her voice. I don't always understand what I should say or shouldn't have said.

Sammy comforted Butchie and Stephanie, "We're so sorry you guys had this terrible episode with the old lady and her vicious gerbil," a smile crossing her face.

Suddenly, the Beatles music was on the radio. I was always excited listening to their music. Butchie and Stephanie always liked the Beatles too.

Sammy was asking us, "Man, you guys really like the Beatles, don't you?"

"Yeah, the Beatles are awesome!" Stephanie bellowed.

Butchie responded, "Yeah!"

While we were having our lunch, I was still thinking about the movie-based fantasy with Sammy. In my thoughts, Sammy is riding a horse through a beautiful forest like in the fairy tales. The waitress bringing our food bill to the table interrupted my dream.

At first, Butchie, Stephanie and I thought she was paying for the food, but Sammy said I should pay, much to my dismay, because she is teaching me how to be independent. I said I didn't think it was fair for me to pay for the four of us.

Finally, Butchie took out his wallet, got the credit card and said, "It's okay, Shorty. Let's split the bill in half."

I replied, "Sounds good to me, Butchie."

****

Outside of the Teammates, Victor and Billy were having a problem with the guys who had thought they were girls. When they heard Victor and Billy's voices, they suddenly realized they were guys. They got really angry, probably because they were embarrassed, and punched and kicked Victor and Billy. Thank God a car was coming and their attackers ran off.

"Guess I now know what being a woman is like," Billy stated. "Those guys really wanted to hit on us. Beautiful women get a lot of unwanted attention."

Victor responded, "Yeah. Tell me about it. They sure were angry when they realized we were guys." Victor saw us through the Teammates window.

At first, Billy was confused why his brother stopped talking. "Dude, what's up?"

Victor whispered, "Billy, come here."

Victor tries to come up with a plan to spy on us.

"Aw come on, Vic." Billy complains, "You always come up with plans, why can't I!"

Victor responded, "Because you're the biggest idiot in the history of mankind."

They argue until Billy decides that a footrace should decide. The winner gets to decide the plan.

Billy beat Victor in a race by distracting him and then pushing him down. "Aw, Billy, that is stupid!" Victor said as he is waving his hand.

Billy gloats that he gets to come up with the plan; much to Victor's disappointment. "So what's your stupid plan, Billy?"

Billy decided that they should dress like clowns to make us laugh. This annoys Victor, who reminds Billy that he hates clowns. Billy explained that everybody loves clowns and it will make me forget about Sammy. Victor is a little annoyed by this. They put the clown outfits over their clothes.

Just as they were about to jump out, a bunch of children suddenly came up to them. "I want a balloon animal."

One child said. "I want you to juggle."

Another child said. "And I want to honk your nose."

A third child said. "And I want a puppy balloon."

As we left the Teammates, we saw a bunch of kids chasing after them. Sammy figured out who the clowns were and she decided we should not get involved with them.

I said to her as I chuckled, "Kids, always have wild imagination."

Sammy rolled her eyes.

The Hamilton Brothers were running for their lives again, "Ahhh!! Get away from us!!"

While they were once again running, Victor stated sarcastically, "Nice plan, Billy!!"

Annoyed by Victor's sarcasm, Billy responded, "Aw shut up!"

****

As we were walking down the street and turned the corner to go to Uptown Comics, we accidentally bumped into someone.

"Oh, sorry sir." I said.

The man turned out to be Robin Williams.

We were surprised to see him. "Sorry we bumped into you, Mr. Williams."

Williams joked as he turned back and forth, "My father is here? Where? Where?"

We responded with a hysterical laugh. I asked Williams, "So when is your next performance, Robin?"

He explained that he'd be starring in a Disney movie that will be coming out next year. You all probably know what I'm talking about. We all told Mr. Williams what big fans we are of his work, and then said goodbye to Williams.

We all walked to the Uptown Comics and got some things that we needed. Sammy reminded us not to get too many comics.

"Oh come on, Sammy," I responded. "We're just getting some things that we really want. Ain't that right, guys?"

Butchie and Stephanie agreed with me. "Yeah, there's quite a few comics I need to catch up on," said Butchie. Sammy is not as crazy about comic books as I am. I explained about how I started getting comics. I've been getting comics since I was 10 years old. They can be pretty exciting. Sammy was concerned about money while I was not. I told Sammy that money does crazy things to people. She agreed. I don't really understand why money is so important. Sammy said she wants to help me understand money. It's good she kept me on track by not letting me spend too much money.

As soon as we finished getting what we wanted, we went to the register and the same clerk from the other day arrived to check us out. When he finished ringing up our new comics, he gave us the receipt so that Mom will keep track of my money. He also made another statement about being a superhero, which made us curious. We decided however not to ask him any questions because we had to get rolling.

****

Meanwhile, the Hamilton Brothers, who, having failed to get anywhere dressed as women or as clowns, had disguised themselves as ice cream men with fake glasses and mustaches.

They were in an ice cream truck. They stole the truck while the real ice cream man was at the bank. Victor and Billy planned to set a trap for Sammy and me, although they haven't figured out that part yet.

Unfortunately, a bunch of kids once again were chasing after them because they love ice cream.

Victor responded, "Get away from us, you little brats!"

Victor drove the ice cream truck to get away, while Billy and the ice cream went flying towards the back door and some bounced toward the front. The ice cream went all over the Hamilton Brothers.

The children continued chasing after them because they still wanted ice cream. Losing patience, Victor told Billy to open the back door and throw the ice cream at the children. For once, Billy followed instructions and threw the ice cream out the back door. The children were shrieking with fear, but were soon thrilled to get all the free ice cream.

"Whew!" Billy stated, "They're gone."

"Oh thank God," Victor responded. "For a minute there I thought they would tear us to shreds or something."

The ice cream truck was driving by as we were leaving the Uptown Comics. Victor spotted us.

"Remember, Billy," Victor said. "Follow my lead."

Billy replied, "You got it, man."

Victor stopped the truck as Billy fell onto the floor.

Victor said in a deep voice, "Step right up, folks! Get your free ice cream here!"

Butchie, Stephanie and I were all excited for it. Sammy, who is fully aware of the Hamilton Brothers' identities, pretended to fall for it and decided to go for some ice cream, although she was not too sure about what was going to happen.

As soon as we got our ice cream, Brad Braverman showed up. Brad is a friend of mine from high school; he is also friends with Stephanie and Butchie. He is a nice guy, but can be childish, overly excited, annoying, and loud. He often appears out of nowhere and has a way of causing trouble.

Brad approaches the truck, looking for his free ice cream, but he recognizes Victor and Billy from the neighborhood. "Hey," he says with a smile, "remember me? I know you two from the deli where I work. You are the Hamilt..."

"Nah...nah...ya got us confused with somebody else," Victor barks, cutting him off. "I never seen you before." With that he turns to Billy. "Let's move," he shouts as he starts up the truck and drives away quickly. The lurching of the truck knocked Billy to the floor as the truck peeled away.

We felt bad for Brad, and decided to take him to an ice cream store to cheer him up, I introduced him to Sammy.

"Wow!" Brad said loudly. "You're so beautiful!"

Sammy chuckled, "Thank you."

Sammy and Brad were talking nicely, but Brad was dominating the conversation with what seemed like a thousand questions. I whispered to Butchie, "And they say I talk too much."

Butchie nodded.

****

The Hamilton Brothers got out of the ice cream truck after they left us because they did not want to be around Brad.

Victor stated, "Uhh…that kid…he almost ruined everything!"

"I know, right?" Billy responded. "GOD!!!"

"One of these days," Victor complained. "I'm going to scream!" He thought for a minute. "Look," he said to his brother, "we need to figure out a way to get close to these people and learn what they have planned. Otherwise, Shark is gonna put my head on a stick."

"Maybe we could..." Billy jumped in, but was quickly cut off.

"Enough, Billy," Victor shot back. "Hold your tongue! I'm the smart one! I will figure it out."

"Hold your tongue?" Billy answered. "I don't know how to do that! It's all...wet and slippery."

"YOU ARE SUCH A MORON!" Victor screams.

"Ahem!" a voice scared the two. "Huh?"

They slowly turned around. It's the real ice cream man and the children that they left behind earlier. They were not happy. The Hamilton Brothers smiled nervously. While Billy hides "his" ice cream hat behind his back. "Oh uh...hello." Victor said as he giggled nervously. "Uhh...I think this truck belongs to you, Mr. Ice Cream Man...sir. Heh."

The furious ice cream man shouted, "Get them!"

The children ran after them as they shouted, "Yeah!"

Victor and Billy said together, "Uh oh!"

After we gave Brad some ice cream, we were heading out and saw that a bunch of children were at the ice cream truck getting ice cream. We had ice cream already. Brad wanted some more so he pushed through the children. Butchie, Stephanie, Sammy and I decided to leave him alone.

As Brad went to the ice cream stand near the truck, he found out that Victor and Billy, who were beaten up, were working for the ice cream man for a day. This was their punishment for stealing the ice cream truck in the first place. They were forced to fill all the ice cream orders while the ice cream man took the orders. As Brad was saying what ice cream he wanted, Billy and Victor both sighed. They felt lucky they didn't go to jail for stealing the ice cream truck.

****

We said good-bye to Butchie and Stephanie and Sammy and I went home. Mom left my clean clothes in my room and Sammy was going to help me fold them and put them in the drawers.

I excused myself to the bathroom. Mom talked to Sammy. Mom thanked Sammy for helping me become more independent.

Sammy responded, "Well I'm just trying my best too."

Mom explained to her that sometimes I could be really difficult.

Sammy nodded as my Mom asked, "So how did you get Shorty to let you go into his room? He usually goes insane if anyone goes in there. He's afraid someone might throw something away. God, the garbage that kid keeps!!!"

Sammy explained to Mom that she just stood there and let me throw away things that aren't worth saving. Sammy said she was interested in listening to my story on how I became a huge Beatles fan. Sammy said she really liked all the Beatles things in my room.

Mom said as Sammy giggled, "Oh, he just LOVES the Beatles. It must be because I told him about how all the girls acted when the Beatles first came to America, everyone fainting and screaming and all."

Mom wrote a list of what we have done today to keep track. As I exited the bathroom door, Mom said she was leaving to get her nails polished and reminded us that we had to fold my clothes neatly. I got annoyed with her comment.

I complained, "Mom!"

Sammy agreed with her. "Let's just get it done Shorty. Why crab about it?"

I tried to fold them my own way, but she helped me. "No, no, no, no, no, no, no, no, no, Shorty. That's not how you fold clothes."

Her comment aggravated me. I understand she's trying to help, but it can be annoying when people always correct me. Sammy did not criticize me in a bad way, but it's still frustrating.

I explained, "I gotta tell ya, Sammy. These guidance and training stuff, i...i...it's like a dictatorship."

She taught me that work should never feel like jail and being told what to do gives us guidance and helps us grow. Sammy told me and showed me how to fold clothes properly. I talked about how sometimes my clothes can be really tricky. I also said that there's not just one correct way to do things. Why isn't my way any good? Sammy said that the important thing was for the clothes to be smoothed out when they come out of the dryer. Folding can be done lots of different ways. She said she was just going to show me how she did things because that's what has worked for her. I said that maybe I will come up with a way that works for me.

Sometimes, I focus on things that aren't real or what I'm facing in reality. It's a way of protecting myself from facing things I don't want to. I was wondering about swearing, even though I don't swear.

I said to Sammy, "I don't even get why people swear."

Sammy replied, "What do you mean?"

I explained to her that people have been swearing for thousands of years and I don't get how they can say these words.

Sammy properly guesses, "Maybe that's just their way of getting angry. I curse sometimes when I'm ticked off."

I reminded Sammy, "You don't swear at me."

Sammy responded, "Of course not."

I wisecracked Sammy, "Yeah, I'm a soft cuddly teddy bear."

She laughed, "You definitely are."

When we finished folding my clean clothes, we brought the basket to my room and put things away in my dresser: one side for the pants and the other side for the shirts. As soon as we finished putting clothes in my drawers, we left my room (although I did let Sammy out first, "After you.") and went to the TV room. We sat down, relaxed, and watched some cartoons on a VHS tape.

I expressed my reactions to some of the scenes in the cartoon. It fascinates me when a character seems to die and then magically comes back to life. Sammy agreed with me.

"Wouldn't it be cool if that happened in real life?" I asked.

Sammy replied, "Yep!"

It's nice to have someone to talk to about cartoons and other things that interest me. We share different opinions and talk about our favorite parts and share what we would change. While Sammy and I were watching the movie, a song played and she was singing along with the lyrics. I was really surprised that her singing voice is so soothing and beautiful.

As soon as the song was over, I was thinking if she could sing, I could be a guitarist. I pressed pause.

"That was amazing, Sammy," I said softly. "Why didn't you tell me about this earlier?"

"Well, Shorty," She explained, "this is kind of embarrassing. I never sang in front of anyone."

I responded, "Well I will always be your biggest fan, Sammy."

"Awww! Thanks, Shorty." Sammy said.

"I was thinking we can try to write a song after the movie, what do you say?" I explained.

"Of course, Shorty." Sammy replied.

After the movie was over, Sammy said, "I think it's that time, Shorty."

"What?" I responded, "but what about our song that we planned for?"

"Yeah, I know." Sammy reminded me that she has a busy schedule. "First, I have to go to my job at CVS. Then, I have a forensics class tomorrow that I have to prepare for. Maybe next time."

Even though I was really disappointed, I knew I had to understand. I stated what my father always taught me every time he came home from work, "Work is not play."

Sammy agreed and got her coat.

I pointed out, "Um, Sammy."

Sammy asked as she was about to exit the door, "Yes, Shorty?"

"I wanted to apologize for being such a pain about the comic book money thing today."

Sammy forgave me because she explained that we all have challenges and differences. "But you can't always get everything you want."

I also explained that I could be stubborn if things don't go the way I want them to.

Sammy replied, "Well we can do things your way, but sometimes it's good to try things my way. We're a team you and me."

She leaned toward me and shook my hand. I asked her for a hug. She hugged me and we heard her back crack. "Oh man, Shorty. My back needed that cracking!" Sammy exited the door. I was surprised that she hugged me. I danced happily with a funny cartoonish face, sticking my tongue out. I put a hat on my head in a goofy fashion. I was singing and dancing again until Old Man Edward yelled up.

"Hopkins!!" I heard him under my apartment floor, "Stop that jumping!"

"OK, SIR!!!" I screamed back, although I whispered. "Eh shut up, Old Man Edward!"

Mom warned me that not everyone is much of a hugger. They can be uncomfortable about it. Besides, every time I give them a hug, I can easily crack their backs since I'm a big guy. I always consider it as one of my running gags.

****

Meanwhile as Sammy went outside, she ran into my Mom who was just getting back from the nail salon.

"Oh, Sammy, were you just leaving?" Mom asked.

Sammy responded, "Yeah, I gotta go to my job at CVS."

Mom showed Sammy her nails. Sammy was impressed with Mom's newly colored nails. "Oh, they look lovely." Sammy stated. Mom thanked her. Sammy explained that she still had a busy day ahead; she is giving some food to the poor after work at CVS. She also has to study for her forensics class tomorrow.

Mom replied, "That's so sweet, Sammy. I wish Shorty could be as generous as you."

Sammy also talked to Mom about my issues with money. She told her how I kept picking out comic books and had no concern about how much money it all might cost. Mom thinks that she should teach me about why money is important. Mom has always thought I needed to learn about the value of things, but I really have no interest.

Sammy replied, "Sure, Betty. Money would be a good thing for Shorty and me to focus on."

Sammy and Mom said goodbye to each other.

****

When Sammy arrived at CVS she saw Jerome standing at the door and Maureen finishing putting some boxes on shelves.

Sammy said, "Hey, Boss."

Jerome gave her a hug and said, "Samantha! How's my girl?"

Sammy stated, "Good."

Maureen asked Sammy, "Hey, Sammy! What's going on?"

Sammy told Maureen about her time with me today. We shouldn't need to repeat the scene again or shall we? Maureen listened to the entire story.

"That's some adventure you had there, girl." Sammy nodded as Caitlin showed up to get her prescription. The girls greeted Caitlin, as they were happy to see her. Caitlin wanted to tell them that she has good news. She got a part in a play.

"No way!" Sammy and Maureen said together as they congratulated her. Caitlin invited them to come to the show for support a week from today. They promised to do their best to be there, although Sammy gets very overbooked with her everyday activities.

Suddenly, Angie showed up at the door. "S'up, girlfriends!"

Angie "greets" them with a smirk. The girls once again get annoyed with Angie around. Angie insults Sammy again by saying, "Sammy, where's your dorky boyfriend?" Maureen and Caitlin tried to defend Sammy. "Angie, why don't you get a life and leave everyone alone?"

Angie mocked them, "Sheesh, if you lovebirds love each other so much, why don't you just marry each other. Oh, wait, I don't think you two have the right to get married."

Insulted and enraged, Maureen shouted as she shoved Angie against the wall, "How dare you! If you think you have the right to make fun of me and my girls, THINK AGAIN!!!" Sammy was horrified by Maureen's violent reaction. Caitlin was disappointed in both Maureen and Angie. She crossed her arms around and thought, "When will that Angie ever learn that Maureen is somebody you should not mess with?"

"Get off of me!!" Angie shouted back as she pushed Maureen, and left the store, shouting, "You girls are freaks!"

Suddenly, Jerome called out for his daughter. "Maureen. Step into my office." She's always a problem for him. Jerome has discussed with her how inappropriate it is to yell and fight in the store. It could be very upsetting to the customers and other workers. She could also really hurt someone and possibly be sued. They argued while Sammy and Caitlin are both listening through the door.

"What?" Maureen asked in confusion like she didn't do anything wrong.

"Maureen," Jerome said in exasperation. "I can't believe it. I just can't. What were you thinking? Were you thinking? I am running a business here, Maureen. I can't have employees pushing around and roughing up patrons. You really could have hurt that girl Angie. I have told you many times to not upset the customers here."

"I…" Maureen tried to explain.

"What's your answer to that?" Jerome chimed in. "I've been putting up with a lot of your rebellious behavior for a long time, but trying to insult a store patron and shove her against the wall…seriously?"

"I…" Maureen once again tried to explain.

"I don't even know what to do about this, Maureen," Jerome chimed in. "Because every time you have done these things, it always breaks my heart."

Annoyed, Maureen decided to leave the office, "Where do you think you're going, young lady?"

"I thought we were going to have a talk," Maureen murmured. "This isn't a talk. This it you freaking out. So freak out by yourself."

"Get back here this instant, Maureen Myllek!" Jerome shouted.

"You know what really bums me out, Dad?" Maureen replied. "Yes, yes, I did shove Angie against the wall. I did insult her. And you know what? You never asked me why?" Jerome was shocked to hear such a harsh statement. Maureen continued yelling as tears brimmed in her eyes. "I did it because she was insulting Sammy, Caitlin and me for no reason. The girl just came in and always makes fun of us so she could laugh just for the fun of it! And she was going to keep laughing unless someone stopped it. So I stopped it. You look me right in the eye and you tell me I did the wrong thing. You tell me Dad!"

"Maureen, I understand," Jerome said. "But you can't just…"

"Well I'd do it again in a second," Maureen chimed in. "So you might as well fire me, Dad."

"Oh come on, Maureen." Jerome complained as Maureen angrily exited the door, "Don't be like that. Please!"

When they ended the conversation, Jerome sighed in despair, thinking he's failing as a father. Sammy was making sure Jerome was okay. Sammy and Jerome share another father and daughter connection. "You're a great father Jerome. It's good you try to keep Maureen's temper in check." They really care deeply about each other, don't they? Sammy also explained to Jerome that she plans to get some groceries for dinner and give half of it to the poor.

Jerome was deeply touched by her selflessness. "I appreciate your support, Sammy." Jerome said. He then asked Sammy, "And I wish that Maureen saw things the same way."

Jerome didn't want Sammy to tell Maureen that he asked her that question. He said, "Oh boy. I would be in trouble if Maureen heard me say that!"

****

Meanwhile after the exhausted Hamilton Brothers got off the ice cream truck, Victor stated, "God, the ice cream man was a pain in the neck."

"Oh tell me about it, dude," Billy responded. "This guy is the worst!"

They continue complaining until a pretty roller-skating girl passes between them.

They shouted together, "DAAAAAAAAMMMMN!!!!!! That girl is a total babe."

As soon as the girl took a break from roller-skating to get some water, Victor told Billy that he could impress ladies by taking out two weights. Victor was lifting the weights near the girl and he was smiling at her. Trying to get her to like him was not going to work because the girl realizes that he smells and she gets disgusted. She gives Victor some deodorant.

Billy says to the girl, "Thanks. I knew he was smelly one." Victor stops lifting the weights and puts on some deodorant. "So, now I am smelling sweet…" Billy chimed in, "You got any plans tonight?"

The girl responded, "Let me just make it clear. No way…"

Billy answered, "Yeah?"

The girl continued, "And you have a bad haircut."

"Hey, Lady!" Victor shouted as he poured his water on the girl and shouted, "Nobody talks to my brother like that except me!" She growled as she stormed off.

Billy said as he breathed heavily, "Thanks, man."

"Hey! That's what brothers are for, right?" Victor said as Billy smiled.

They decided to get out of there before someone calls the cops. Before they did, the girl came back with her muscular boyfriend, who was holding a crowbar. "That's them, honey!"

The Hamilton Brothers gasped in horror, "These are the idiots that were hitting on me! Beat em' to a pulp!"

Victor yelled, "Run!!!"

The guys ran as the boyfriend angrily screamed, "You Sick Sons of B*$#$%#!!!!"

He ran after them and threw the crowbar at Victor, narrowly missing him by an inch. He then picked up his crowbar and encountered Billy as he pathetically begged for mercy.

"Please don't hurt me with a crowbar, mister!" Billy pleaded, tears welling up in his eyes. "I can do anything you want!"

"Are you crying?" he asked.

"No," Billy answered. He was crying.

The guy felt bad for Billy, so he simply told Billy to stay away from his girlfriend, dropped the crowbar and marched away.

"Well that really went well," Victor said sarcastically.

Billy screamed, "Ow!! What was wrong with that guy! He almost killed me!"

Victor shouted, "Quit your whining, man!"

Suddenly, the Hamilton Brothers spotted Sammy walking out of CVS, carrying some food. They watched her give away some of her groceries to some of the homeless people.

"Oh God bless you, Sammy!" One woman cried, "Bless you!"

"Oh don't worry," Sammy replied. "I think it's only right to share our blessings and offer help through life's difficult journey. I want to be there for others."

"Well I gotta tell you, Sammy," one man replied. "You're an ambassador of compassion."

The Hamilton Brothers realized Sammy is genuinely a good person. Not everybody shares his or her food with the less fortunate. This really touched Victor and Billy as they burst into tears of joy.

"Man," Victor said. "I had no idea Shark's girl would do something so... Nice."

"I know, right?" Billy replied. "It's like you get to know somebody for the very first time."

They are starting to question their loyalty to Shark.

Remember, Kids. Being smart or dumb is one thing, but what really matters is having a moral compass and knowing what is right or wrong.

Suddenly, a hand tapped Billy's shoulder. It was their angry mother, much to their surprise. They tried to explain everything, but she refused to listen and pulled their ears. "You boys are in so much trouble when we get home." They were screaming in pain.

"Ow! Ow! Ow! Ow! Ow! Ow! Ow! Ow! Ow! Ow! Ow! Ow! Ow! Ow1 Ow! Ow!"

Lesson Learned: A girl or boy might be pretty or handsome on the outside. But on the inside, there could be the ones who are cold, selfish and mean. If they're trying to insult you, don't let them make you feel that way. It might look like you're walking towards heaven. But it's really like walking into a trap when you meet a girl or boy like that. Physically beautiful and mentally ugly. If you fall in love with people like that don't do it. Try to find someone who is nice, honest and caring. Physical appearance doesn't matter as long as someone is mentally beautiful, aka pure of heart.

****

Sammy returned home after work. Joan already put the dishes on the table and Mikey was eating his dinner.

Sammy said, "Hello, Nana. How are you?"

Joan replied, "Oh I'm fine, dear."

When Sammy's grandmother asked how her day was, she responded it was "the usual" and hugged her grandmother while yawning.

While they were having dinner, Sammy explained to her grandmother that before she went home from work, she spent her time among the less fortunate, bringing them food.

"You should see the look on their faces when someone helps them." Sammy said.

Joan felt so proud to have a generous granddaughter. Joan asked Sammy if she could talk with her privately. She did not want to talk about me in front of Mikey.

Joan is still concerned that I might be another pig like Shark. They get into a heated argument once they enter Joan's room. Sammy tried to convince Joan that I might have some issues, but I would never do anything awful to her.

Joan complained, "I just don't want you to get hurt, Sammy! You can be quite naive and trusting. What if Shorty is some sort of psychopath like that Shark guy was?!"

Shorty shouts, "Nana!!"

Joan continues to complain, "You're still not ready for this!"

"Nana!!" Sammy once again shouts, "I feel like a new person when I'm with him. We're not dating Nana. I am his comm. hab. worker. I get paid to spend time with him..."

Joan chimed in, "Samantha!! I'm still very concerned about you."

Sammy was shocked. Joan calms herself, as she hates being so hard on her beloved granddaughter.

Joan explained to Sammy in a melancholy tone, "I'm sorry, puppet. It's just that the night your parents perished, a part of me died with them, but for the last eight agonizing years, I've vowed to be a good parent to you and Mikey no matter what it takes. It also breaks my heart to see you getting beaten up by this monster Shark. Now that you're seeing somebody else, it really bothers me to say this, dear."

Joan sighed in an emotional way, "I have no choice but to forbid you from getting involved with this young man. As long as I'm still standing, I need to keep you safe."

Horrified, Sammy once again tried to complain, "Nana!!"

"And know this," Joan interrupts, "this will be the last time for me to warn you about getting involved with any men. Is that understood?"

"No, Nana," Sammy replied. "You're wrong about Shorty! He's a good guy who has a nice family and he's nothing like Shark!"

As Sammy tearfully runs off, Joan sadly bends down. Mikey, who was secretly listening to them behind the door, chases after Sammy and comforts her as she cries.

Mikey asked, "What's wrong, Sammy?"

"I just don't get it." Sammy sniffled sadly. "Why can't Nana just respect me enough to let me make my own decisions?"

"I don't know," Mikey replied. "But I don't think it matters what Nana has to say, I think Shorty is a cool guy. He took us to see Beauty and the Beast and we had pizza with him. I think you should hang out with him more.

Surprisingly, Mikey was supportive to her rather than teasing her like he usually does. "Thank you for understanding, Mikey," Sammy said as they hugged. Joan secretly watched the whole thing through a little opening in the door. She smiled when they hugged.

Sammy and Mikey having an emotional brother and sister moment, how sweet.

****

Mrs. Hamilton was very angry with her boys for running away from her and causing mayhem all over town. The Hamilton Brothers' punishment was that they would have to go without dinner. One of them tried to make an excuse to leave.

"But, Ma!" Victor cried. "I'm really hungry."

"Yeah." Billy said.

"If you two are going to act like children I am going to treat you like children," Mrs. Hamilton roared. "Now go to your room!"

"But, Ma!" Victor protested. "That's not fair!"

"I don't give a rat's rear!" Mrs. Hamilton responded, grabbing the remote and turning the TV off. "Let's go, children!"

Victor rose to his feet, tired and defeated. "But Vic," Billy said, "we ain't kids no more."

"Oh, yes you are mister," their mother shot back. She looked Billy right in the eye. "Now get movin', and make it snappy!"

Billy, too, gave up, and the two men, browbeaten into submission, shuffled off to their room. Once settled in, they decided to call Shark and update him about my time with Sammy so far.

****

At his lair, Shark was standing at his fireplace, praying to the Virgin Mary (whom he addresses as "Beata Maria", meaning "Blessed" in Latin). He asked Mary for help to win back "his" angel and make me burn in hell. He was singing about his lust for Sammy, his own holiness, and his hatred of "God's mistakes," which includes me.

I gotta tell ya, this song he is singing sounds pretty scary that it is depicting hell, damnation, the Catholic religion, and lust. Be careful with fireplaces kids. Lots of villains stand near fireplaces, plotting their evil deeds.

However, his phone rings, which really gets him angry as he growls. "What is it this time?" Shark yelled as he picked up the phone.

Billy wanted to tell him, "Boss, we want you to know that..."

"I'll handle this," Victor chimed in. "Shark, we want you to know that Hopkins lives in the same joint as us."

"Yeah," Billy agreed. "He does."

"Hmm," Shark puzzled. "Interesting."

"Yeah, yeah." Victor exclaimed. "but just one question, how come you still haven't told us what you have in mind for Hopkins and your girl, Boss?"

"Because, my friends," Shark replied. "This is something you two wouldn't understand. Besides, when the time comes, you'll know. In the meantime, you two keep following Hopkins and Samantha to find out what's going on between them."

Confused, Victor and Billy decided to go along with it.

"Okay, Boss," Victor said. "Maybe I'll come up with a plan to get in touch with them. Billy here would just want to try the same old things over and over again."

"Hey," Billy chimed in. "You always get to decide everything around here, but why can't I? Besides, I got a condition!"

"Because, like I said before, Billy," Victor argued. "You're the biggest idiot in the history of mankind."

"ENOUGH!!!!" Shark barked into the phone. "It doesn't matter who comes up with a plan as long as you two do as I say."

Billy gloated at Victor by blowing a raspberry at him, much to Victor's annoyance.

"Now, my friends," Shark continued. "Since my last encounter with them, it appears that Samantha and Hopkins are starting to become closer. So maybe until Christmas comes, you two will just do as I say and I will do God's will. I will then show my eternal passion for Samantha and let Hopkins feel the touch of hell's fire as he dies."

This insane speech really confused the Hamilton Brothers, but they decided they better pretend to go along with whatever Shark was saying.

"Oh don't worry, man," Victor replied. "We, the Hamilton Brothers, will...uh...do this thing and uhhh...we won't let you down."

"Yeah," Billy chimed in. "and we can...uhh...try to get in touch with that Hopkins guy and your girl for you, dude."

"Besides," Victor continued. "they won't know what'll hit him, man."

"Good," Shark said evilly. "then proceed with my plan. Just keep watching them and report back to me. When Christmas comes, the day the Son of God was born, I will have my revenge on Hopkins and finally... Samantha and I will be whole again."

****

As time went by, Sammy and I were spending more and more time together. We learned a lot of things from each other. Our relationship grew and we became good friends. I was doing everything I could to help her while she was helping me to manage my emotions better. We were going out together often. We enjoy each other's company.

Although we had some disagreements about following the "rules", we learned to accept our differences. For example, Sammy was concerned about money while I was not. Also, I don't always follow instructions like I should. I need to pay more attention instead of focusing on fantasy.

Sometimes I can get a little irrational, but I didn't want to interfere with my time with Sammy. She helped me learn how to control myself. Sammy also taught me this big lesson, "Don't rush through tasks. If you rush things you are more likely to mess up and have to repeat things over again. It is better to do something once the right way than to rush through things and have to do it over and over again."

Sammy really likes sports and I liked going to the movies. I told Sammy that money does crazy things to people. She agreed. I understand that money is important. She is very respectful.

We went to the gym and she helped me make healthy food choices. Sammy helped me understand money and overall kept me on track. She also helped me see reality. Sammy taught me that opposites attract.

I even treated Mikey like a little brother I never had like I did with Georgie. Joan still doesn't trust me, because she thinks that every man is like Shark. She doesn't even know me, but she is just worried about Sammy.

Whenever Sammy felt sad, I always tried to make her smile and laugh. We even gave each other gifts and watched cartoons and movies together. Our friendship became closer and more affectionate.

Sammy helped me learn to do my own laundry, clean my bedroom, organize my comic books, and keep track of my possessions. She is also a very reliable young woman and is eager to help me learn independent living skills.

We go shopping together after we make a list of what we need and where we should go. We look at movie times in the newspaper and decide where to go.

Sammy also took me to her apartment sometimes. I was impressed with her bedroom. I also discovered she had a record player and lots of albums. We played music and danced together. Sammy and I also made a song and we worked on it for weeks. Sammy is the singer and I'm a guitarist.

Sammy was aware that the Hamilton Brothers were following us. She is doing her best to ignore them. Every time Victor and Billy secretly spied on us under Shark's order, they got thrown out into different dumpsters. They used absurdly complex contraptions and elaborate plans to pursue their "prey." Their devices comically backfired. The Hamilton Brothers often were injured in slapstick fashion like Wile E. Coyote chasing the Roadrunner.

One time, they disguised themselves as construction workers working at a nearby construction site. From there they used binoculars to watch us through a window in my living room. They would scramble down whenever we two left the building and follow us wherever we went, taking notes along the way so that they could report back to Shark. Two days in a row, while Victor was watching us, Billy stepped in a bucket of cement; the second day he tried to get Victor's help, but Victor was preoccupied with the task at hand. He told Billy to "Wait a minute, will ya?" while he barked out observations for Billy to write down. When he finally stopped, he looked over to see his idiot brother standing there with one foot in the cement bucket. "C'mon, you idiot," Victor said, "let's report in with Shark."

"I can't Victor," Billy answered, a whimper in his voice. Victor looked at him, bemused. "Because?" he shot back.

"'Cause my foot is stuck," Billy responded. Victor shook his head and walked over to find that the cement had actually dried and hardened around Billy's foot. "YOU IDIOT!" he shouted.

Victor looked around for a way to get his idiot brother's foot loose from the cement. "I should try TNT," he mumbled to himself. He finally settled on the answer: a large sledgehammer that was leaning against a wall. "This will do the job," he said, picking it up. It was really heavy.

Victor dragged the large tool over to his brother. "Now, listen up, baby brother," he said. "Here is how this will work. You will hold your leg and foot really still, and I will lift the sledgehammer up over my head and slam the head onto the cement, and that'll break the cement into a hundred pieces. Then you walk away."

Billy was not pleased. "Whaddaya mean slam? I don't like slam." Victor told him it was the only way to free him, but Billy was still unsure.

"If you get to slam me with a hammer, I get to slam you with a hammer," said Billy. "Then we're even." But Victor was having none of it. "Tell you what," he answered. "If I get my foot stuck in a bucket of cement, you can hit me in the head with a sledgehammer."

"Deal," Billy almost jumped up. "You gotta deal!"

"K," Victor said, "Now hold still." Victor gathered all his strength and raised the sledgehammer up over his head, as Billy whimpered next to him. Victor closed his eyes and swung the sledge as hard as he could. Unfortunately for him, his brother flinched and moved his foot just enough for Victor to miss his target and slam into his own leg. Pain shot through his entire body. "AAAAAAAHHHHHHHHH! AAAHHHHHHHHHH!" Victor roared as he fell to the ground. "I THINK I BROKE MY LEG!!!!!!" he screamed. "YOU IDIOT! YOU IDIOT! YOU IDIOT!"

After a few minutes the pain finally began to go away. Victor tried but it was very difficult to stand; his leg was throbbing in pain. He looked at his brother, anger in his eyes.

"Ya know, Vic," Billy said. "Ya missed. I still got the bucket on my foot."

"I HATE YOU!" Victor roared. "You are such an idiot." He walked away, but quickly realized that he really had no choice but to try again. "What am I gonna do," he thought to himself, "tell my mother that her youngest is gonna go through life with a bucket for a foot?"

Victor grabbed the sledgehammer again and snuck up on Billy. He raised the tool up over his head, gathered all his strength and swung.

A loud boom rang out as the sledgehammer made contact, and the chunk of cement that had surrounded Billy's foot exploded, with pieces firing out in all directions. Billy was free! "Thanks, bro'" Billy said, smiling again. "You saved me."

He had just gotten the words out of his mouth when the two brothers heard a roar from their left. They looked over and saw an enormous man, a construction worker, bleeding from the head and looking everywhere. "HEY, YOU TWO," he barked. "Are you the two idiots who threw the cement at me?" He reached down and picked up a big chunk of cement, and held it out.

"WELL, WHO DID THIS?" he screamed, rage in his voice. The two brothers looked at one another, and then back at the injured "co-worker." Victor pointed across the site to a spot about 20 feet away. "That guy," he said, "in the blue shirt, over there." The man turned, and the two brothers ran off as fast as they could, but both limping while they ran.

How stupid these guys are, huh?

While they were spying on Sammy and me, the Hamilton Brothers were starting to realize how kind and courageous she is. They weren't too sure if they could work for Shark any longer.

****

At holiday time in December, we were invited to a Christmas/Hanukkah party at the Teammates for people with disabilities. I invited Sammy, Mikey, Maureen, and Caitlin to come to the party and promised the people at Teammates that Sammy and I would sing the song we made for the party.

Butchie and I got dressed in our FAAAAAAAANCYYYY tuxedos. We were watching one of our favorite Christmas movies of all time, Home Alone. I imitated the crazy old man Johnny who has a gun and Butchie imitated the greedy gangster Snakes. We crack ourselves up, imitating the scene where Johnny shoots Snakes and says, "Keep the change you filthy animal." They were dressed up too so when we dress up, we always think of them and laugh at ourselves.

Old Man Edward yells from the floor below, "Will you two pipe down?!"

I whispered, "How about I give you the change if you SHUT UP, YOU FILTHY ANIMAL!"

Butchie echoed, "Yeah, you filthy animal!" We laughed and gave each other a high five. "We totally crack ourselves up," I said. Butchie replied, "Yeah."

Mom knocked on the door. "Boys, we better go." I stopped the movie and we opened the door.

Mom said, "Well don't you guys look handsome."

I said, "Thanks, Mom."

There was a knock on the door. It was Stephanie in a beautiful dress. Butchie was happy to see Stephanie. "Whoa, Babe. You look great."

"Merry Christmas, Darling," Stephanie said as she happily ran to Butchie and they embraced.

"Merry Christmas to you too, Babe." Butchie replied as they kissed.

Mom and I were both weirded-out and uncomfortable about seeing them making out in front of us. I whispered to Mom, "They definitely need to get a room." Mom nodded and laughed. We were all getting ready for the party. Diane could not come because she had a very important meeting.

Mom gave me a corsage for Sammy. It looked like a flower in a glass cup, so pretty.

"Wow, it looks so beautiful, Mom." I said.

Mom reminded me, "Don't forget your guitar, Shorty."

"Thanks for reminding me, Mom," I replied, as I went back to my room to get my guitar. I was taking too long to search for my guitar. Mom was losing patience. She was about to scream my name to get my attention, but lucky for me I found the guitar and got to the door before she started screaming.

"Sometimes, it's hard to get you out the door, Shorty." Mom said.

"And sometimes, it's hard to go places with your complaining, Mom." I replied. Mom sighs in response and rolls her eyes at me.

****

Meanwhile, the Hamilton Brothers were outside in the bushes, waiting for us to come out.

"Come on, man," Billy complained. "We've been out here for hours. When will they…?"

"Shhh!!!!" Victor interrupted quietly, "They're coming." They hid in the bushes as we went out the door, chatting.

As we were walking toward Sammy's apartment, the Hamilton Brothers secretly followed us until they bumped into a tough guy, who is the comic book clerk. He easily recognized them as the carjackers who crashed his car. The clerk punched them and threw them into the dumpster.

"Oh no!" The boys yelled as they went flying towards the dumpster, "Not again!" They slammed into the lid and fell into the dumpster as the lid shut down.

The clerk shouted, "That's for stealing my car and smashing it up, Punks! You're lucky I don't have time to clobber you some more." He then stormed off.

****

Sammy, Maureen, and Caitlin were getting ready to go to the dance. They were having some girl talk. Sammy went to help Mikey dress in his little FANCY tuxedo, although he did bravely try to fight it at first. Mikey didn't like to get dressed FANCY.

Maureen said as she showed Caitlin, who is wearing contacts for the dance, her new outfit, "And that ladies and gentlemen is why I'm the champion of fashion!"

"Wow, Maureen!" Caitlin replied. "You look astonishing."

"Well, Cat." Maureen explained, "That's what the party is about. Being astonishing for you."

"I gotta say, girlfriend." Caitlin replied. "You picked the right dress."

Maureen and Caitlin were laughing until Sammy came through her bedroom door.

"Sorry about that," Sammy said. "Mikey is still complaining about putting on a tuxedo."

"Well you know what they say about little brothers, girl," Maureen explained. "They're a major pain in the rear."

Suddenly, Joan showed up and asked, "Excuse me, Sammy. May I talk to you outside of your room?"

Sammy replied, "Sure, Nana."

Sammy left her bedroom to talk to her grandmother. Maureen and Caitlin were concerned for Sammy.

"The poor girl," Maureen stated. "Always being controlled by her granny."

"Well, Maureen," Caitlin reminded Maureen. "She's just being overprotective about her grandchildren because she loves them. Besides you know how hard it is for Sammy, right?"

"Of course I do, Cat." Maureen replied. "But we're her best friends and we look after her no matter what."

"I know, Maureen. I know," Caitlin sighed as she suddenly heard loud voices outside of Sammy's room. "Shh!!! Listen." Maureen and Caitlin overheard Sammy's argument with Joan.

"Nana!!" Sammy complained. "I've already made my decision and I'm not talking about this anymore!"

"Tell him you're sick," Joan panics. "Tell him that you've changed your mind."

Sammy shouted, "Why can't you just be happy for me?! He's a nice guy from a nice family and he is only a friend."

Joan replied, "Well, it's just that I love you so much and I don't want you to get hurt, dear."

"Look, Nana," Sammy said as she turns and walks away, "Don't ruin this for me. Everyone I meet is not going to be like Shark. There are some genuinely nice people out there."

"Look, Sammy," Joan tried to make another excuse to make Sammy stay, "I'll tell him that…"

"Nana, Mikey and I are going and that's final!" Sammy shouted, "And you're not going to say another word about it!"

Sammy went back to her room while Joan sadly bent her head down, still concerned for her grandchildren's safety, although she hates being too hard on them.

As soon as Sammy got back to her room, Maureen and Caitlin were both pretending they didn't hear anything.

"So Sammy?" Maureen asked. "What were you doing out there?"

"Well you know my grandmother," Sammy replied. "Sometimes she doesn't understand."

Mikey needed help tying his shoes. Sammy helped him. Her grandmother watched her and said, "You all look fantastic, dear. I hope you have a wonderful time, but above all else, please be careful. Christmas is such a beautiful time of year to get together with family and friends."

"Thanks for understanding, Nana." Sammy said.

"Yeah, Nana." Mikey said.

"We'll be home early," Sammy said as she kissed her grandmother on the cheek. "I love you, Nana."

After everyone went out the door, Joan thought to herself. "Like I said, that girl better be careful."

****

When we arrived at Sammy's apartment building, Mikey, Maureen and Caitlin came out the door and they acted like stage announcers.

"Ladies and gentlemen," Maureen said. "May we present, Sammy Johnson!"

Sammy came out in a really beautiful red dress. I was very impressed with her new, dressed up look. It's like she transformed from this little girl into an ultimate beauty queen like Cinderella.

"Oh!!" Mom over-enthusiastically said about Sammy's dress. "Sammy, what a gorgeous dress! You look beautiful!"

"You do." Stephanie agreed.

"Thank you." Sammy replied.

Stephanie replied, which annoys Mom, "Well not as beautiful as me but yeah."

"Wow, Sammy!" I said, "You look like an angel."

"Thanks, Shorty," Sammy responded. "That was sweet." I gave her the corsage, which she loved, and she put it on her dress, just above her heart.

We stared at each other for a second until Stephanie interrupted. She put her arms around us, "Come on, guys, we have partying to do."

"Wahoo!" Stephanie shouted. "It's party time!"

As we were all walking, Sammy and I looked at the stars. It made me think about that famous song from "Disney's Pinocchio", "When You Wish Upon A Star." I explained to Sammy about making wishes on the stars. Sammy became depressed when she remembered her late parents since she used to watch the stars with her parents.

"Listen to me, I know it's still rough for you without your parents, but just be strong about this, OK?"

I haven't told anybody this, but I told Sammy, "When the sky turns nighttime it's like nature somehow tried to show us that when the sun went down, it's like nighttime tries to show us a microscopic version of the universe, probably the Earth's view on it."

Sammy was confused about my comment and explained correctly, "I think you mean when the sun goes down it's like nature tries to show us a microscopic version of the universe. It's as though nighttime gives us the Earth's view of space. At night, we see all the stars and we feel like a very small part of the universe."

"Wow," I said. "You really know how to say things better than I do. I'm glad you understood what I was trying to say."

"Thank you, Shorty." Sammy replied as I blushed.

I gotta tell you guys, the way Sammy and I were dressed beautifully and walking to a fancy dance, it's like the romantic scenes in the classic movies if you know what I mean.

****

Meanwhile, Victor and Billy got out of the dumpster once again and everyone was staying away from them because they both smelled really bad. Everyone passing by them on the sidewalk pinched their noses and said, "PEEEEUUUUU!!!!!"

The Hamilton Brothers blamed each other for losing us and they fought by slapping each other like children until Victor saw us walking by and reminded Billy about their mission. So they followed us again. We finally made it to the Teammates where there are beautiful Christmas and Hanukkah decorations everywhere. We all got in except for the Hamilton Brothers. The hostess refused to let them in because they smelled so bad.

"I don't stink," Victor explained. "My brother here is the one who stinks."

Billy shouted, "Do not!"

Victor shouted, "Do too!"

Billy shouted, "Do not!"

Victor shouted, "Do too!"

As they continued their fight, the hostess pressed the button under the desk. The security guard grabbed them by their shirts and threw them into the dumpster.

Inside the dumpster, Victor thought they should wait for us to get out of the restaurant, but Billy said, as he sniffed himself, "As soon as we wash ourselves."

Victor was going to remind Billy about the mission Shark gave them, but then he decided to follow Billy's lead because he didn't want to be in the dumpster all night like last time. The Hamilton Brothers got out of the dumpster as they argued about who gets to take a shower first when they got home.

Victor saw the river nearby, and an idea popped into his head. He thought in order to keep track of their mission, they could take a bath in the river. Billy was confused at first, "I don't get it, Dude."

Victor explained what he had in mind. Billy felt uncomfortable about this but decided to go along with it. They took off their clothes while no one was looking.

While they were cleaning themselves, the same kids from the ice cream incident came along and stole their clothes, threw them in the dumpster and they hid behind the bushes. Good payback for what they had done to the kids. When the Hamilton Brothers got out, they realized their clothes are gone. They looked everywhere, and it took them almost an hour to find them...hidden in the dumpster right next to the one they had been in! The kids laughed and laughed.

Hiding in the shadows and behind the dumpsters, Victor and Billy both got their clothes back on. Billy just finished tying his shoe when the trouble-making kids returned.

"So you dorks got your clothes back." Kevin said disappointedly, "Congratulations."

"Yeah, that's right, son!" Victor teased as Billy does the raspberry, "Looks like we win this time."

"Yeah!!" Billy agrees with Victor. "Do you little squirts think you can mess with the Hamilton Brothers?! I DON'T THINK SO!!"

"Oh woo-hoo!" Kevin said sarcastically. "Well let me respond to that."

Kevin "responded" by blowing a raspberry at Victor and Billy, much to their disgust and the other kids' laughter.

"Ha! Ha! Ha!" Kevin laughed. "Losers!"

As the kids left laughing, the boys got really annoyed.

"Hmmph," Victor said. "Bunch of punks."

"Tell me about it." Billy replied. "Now where were we?"

"Ma really did drop you on your head," Victor said. "Didn't she?"

"Yeah," Billy replied. "many times."

Annoyed, Victor reminded Billy about their "mission" and they try to figure out how to spy on us.

"Hey," Billy said as he pointed at the lighted Christmas bushes. "Let's hide in the bushes over there."

"Billy." Victor said. Billy thinks that he is against the idea, and is pleasantly surprised when Victor says, "That has got to be...the coolest idea ever!!"

They decided to hide in the bushes across the street where the Teammates is, even though the lights on the bushes were too bright. Billy thought they looked beautiful, but the lights blinded Victor. "My eyes", screamed Victor.

****

Inside Teammates, everything was beautiful. There were a lot of holiday decorations: wreaths, a menorah, bows, and a giant tree. We took our table. It was table #1. Butchie, Stephanie and I chatted with each other about things we had on our minds like movies and comic books.

Everybody else wanted to talk about other things like politics, Christmas shopping, and their health concerns. Butchie and Stephanie eventually got into other people's conversations, much to my dismay.

"So, Shorty." Caitlin said. "Sammy told us that you guys are going to do a song for the party later."

"Yes," I said. "All my life, I always say things rather than doing things. Luckily, Sammy helped me with that. Sammy and I wrote a song together. Writing songs really helps me understand my feelings about lots of different things. I don't want to reveal the name of the song, but I'll tell you one thing, Sammy is the singer and I'm the guitarist."

While we were having dinner, some old friends of mine came by to say hello. "Hey, Shorty. Long time no see," Rick Parker said. He helps his younger brother and another friend of mine named Bobby Parker, who was injured in a car accident and uses a wheelchair.

Bobby said, "Yo, Shorty, What's up? Merry Christmas." Then he started to rap, "I don't want to diss-miss. I want to kiss your lips that is filled with Swiss-miss, hot chocolate, putting candy cane in my pocket, it's Bobby Koocher." As he was rapping, everyone felt awkward about it. We all knew, even though I don't always "get" these things, it was a little weird.

Rick shouted, "Stop it, Bobby! Stop it! Stop it!"

Bobby talked back, "Shut up!!"

Rick said, "Bobby!!" Bobby crossed his arms in anger.

Rick asked, "So, what have you guys been up to?"

"Oh nothing much, guys." I replied. Rick automatically assumed that Sammy is my girlfriend. Sammy and I dismissed it. "Absolutely not!" I said. Sammy said, "No. No. No. No. That's not true. We're just friends."

I explained, "This is Sammy Johnson. She actually works for me as my com-hab worker. We're also going to perform for a show tonight."

"Wow! That's awesome." Rick replied. "Good work, man. Get it done."

"Well good luck on this thing, Shorty." Bobby chimed in.

Rick's crazy stepbrother, Nick Roman comes in and shouted, "RIIIICK!!"

"Sheesh, man." Rick replied. "What's your problem?"

"The problem I'm having is that one of these days, Rick." Nick said with his comedic voice, or as he liked to call it, his "emphasis" voice, "You're going to make me BLOW MY STACK!!!!!"

Rick asked. "Why?"

Nick said. "In case you have forgotten, you, Bobby and I are supposed to go on STAGE NOW!!!"

"Well we gotta go, Shorty." Rick said. "It's been nice seeing you. Let's get together."

"Peace out, yo!" Bobby shouted.

After Rick, Nick and Bobby left to go on stage and entertain us, Ace and Gloria came to my table to greet us.

"Well!!" Gloria said. "The gang's all here!!"

"Hey, Gloria." Ace joked. "That's my line!!"

"Well, Ace." Gloria joked back. "there's always next time."

Ace and Gloria were both overly-enthusiastic about our FANCY clothes and I let them know that Sammy and I are ready for the song we promised to make for the party later. They left to greet more guests.

That evening after dinner, Butchie, Stephanie and I sang one of our favorite songs. During the song, I was swirling around on the dance floor to entertain everyone. Mom was worried that I might have a wardrobe malfunction and humiliate myself.

After the song was over, a slow song came on and Sammy and I waltzed, which reminded me of a classic musical movie. You know the ones, the ones with all the beautiful singing and slow dancing.

When the song was over, Sammy and I decided to sing a song like her mother sang to her when she was little. Her mother made up the songs after reading poetry. She named it "Love Wins." She sang it really well and I played the guitar. Everyone was surprised that Sammy has a voice of an angel, even Mikey, Maureen and Caitlin. The song was really touching.

"Love Wins"

Leaves fall

Dreams end

Fear consumes, but we try to bend

Hope still lives as we try to mend

Silenced children

Sleeping and cold

While they are dreaming dreams of gold

This ship might sink

But we'll stay afloat

Night may fall

But light will come

And we'll keep singing until it's done

Life will come

With the rising sun

For we stay golden

As we live

In the light of God away from sins

For in the end,

Again and again

Fear may consume,

But love wins

God bless the angels

Author's note: "Love Wins" is originally a poem by my second young cousin once removed, Joseph "Joey" Hopkins (2000), as a tribute one year after the tragic Sandy Hook Elementary shooting. I was really impressed with his hard work that I asked him if I could make it into an emotional theme song for Shorty and Sammy and he accepted.

Sammy and I walked outside when the song ended. I gave Sammy my fancy jacket to keep her warm. We had a nice talk about how fun that was and Sammy's amazing singing voice.

"That was fun." Sammy said.

"Well, I'm glad we did this tonight." I replied. "You have the perfect voice of an angel."

"Aw. Thank you, Shorty." Sammy replied.

We were blushing for a second. "I...I wouldn't have done this without you." Sammy said softly.

"Hey," I replied as I placed my hand into hers. "We make a pretty good team you and me."

When I'm having this romantic moment, my heart rate is increasing and it's like in the love stories and movies. Sammy wanted to tell me something. I thought she was going to tell me she loves me.

We nearly kissed, but Stephanie called out that my Mom said it's time to go. We went back into the Teammates to get our belongings.

****

Unknown to us, the Hamilton Brothers, after they got their clothes back on behind the bushes, saw us together.

Billy thought it was sweet, "Aww, that's sweet." Billy said in a "sweet moment tone" like they call it in the sitcom audience recording.

"No you idiot," Victor said. "Shark's girl just kissed Hopkins. We need to report this to Shark immediately."

"But if Shark finds out about this," Billy responded. "he'll kill them."

"I know, man," Victor reminded Billy. "But if we don't tell him, he'll kill us. Now come on!"

As soon as they got out of the bushes, Billy suggested they play a board game, but Victor refuses. "We don't have time for this, Billy."

When Billy asks why not, Victor says that he thinks Billy needs to go to anger management before he plays another board game with him.

In response, Billy hollers at Victor to name one time he has had anger problems.

One time, Billy challenged Victor to bet on a Super Bowl game. Victor takes the 49ers and talks Billy into giving him six points and taking the Broncos. When the 49ers won easily, Billy threw a bottle at Victor and almost hit their mother.

Second time, Victor challenged Billy who can count to ten quicker. Victor immediately starts counting and made it to ten before Billy knew what hit him.

Third time, they were playing a board game. When it was clear Victor was going to win, Billy knocked the table over and went on a rampage. Victor tried to calm him down. "You may not have anger management issues, but you sure are a sore loser."

Billy explains to Victor that the cause of his bad temper was he has always hated losing. Whenever he loses, he freaks out. Billy said a made up word. "Besides you're nothing but a bull twerp!"

Victor says that it wasn't even a word. However, Billy tries to defend himself.

"Oh yeah!" Billy shouted. "Well I think it's the best way to describe you!"

As Billy went to reach Victor, they crashed into a tree, which woke up a hibernating squirrel. It leaped and attacked Victor. When it was about to bite him, Victor grabbed it by the tail and threw it off to the side.

Billy shouted, "Dude, that was awesome!"

Victor yelled, "Shut up and help me get up!!"

As Billy pulled him up, he complained, "Ok, man. Sheesh,"

"Look, Billy." Victor reminded Billy that Sammy and I just "kissed."

"So?" Billy replied.

Exasperated, Victor continued. "So, we need to go, now!" When we got out of the Teammates, the Hamilton Brothers ran off.

****

Meanwhile in his candlelit room at the "Garden of Eden," Shark was standing right at the crooked old window, glaring with a creepy look in his eyes, and he thought about what he had been reading before in his Bible: the Lord's Prayer.

"Our Father who art in heaven, hallowed be your name. Your kingdom come. Your will be done, on Earth as it is in heaven."

Suddenly, the Hamilton Brothers arrived and reported what they just "saw."

Surprisingly, Shark is fully aware of what they're about to say and responded, "You don't need to worry, boys. I got a big God-giving idea that might crucify Hopkins and make Samantha and me whole again."

Victor was confused about what he was talking about at first, but he was starting to realize what Shark meant when he explained how to make himself and Sammy "one." It really disturbs Victor and he wants to talk to Billy about this.

"Uhh, Billy, can I have a word with you?" Victor whispered, "Have you noticed that Shark has gone COMPLETELY INSANE?!"

Billy responded, "Wh...what do you mean?"

Victor explained, "Just look at him."

They look at Shark, saying to himself by quoting, *Ephesians 5:22-24,*

"Wives, submit to your husbands as to the Lord. For the husband is the head of the wife as Christ is the head of the church, his body, of which he is the Saviour. Now as the church submits to Christ, so also wives should submit to their husbands in everything."

Billy was confused at first, "Uh...what is he talking about, dude?"

But when Victor whispered in his ear, "he's crazy man", Billy finally understood what Shark is planning on doing.

"You're right, Vic," Billy cried. "How do we get out of here!"

"Just follow me," Victor responded quietly. "And that way, we sneak ourselves right out the door."

Billy said softly, "Okay."

They tried to escape, but Shark caught them. He catches up with them and once again slapped the Hamilton Brothers with his Bible really hard and pointed a gun at them.

"You two imbeciles are nothing but goddamn cowards!" Shark shouted. "You think you can leave me now?!"

"No, sir." The boys looked at each other and they sadly said together, "We're not."

"Well let me explain something to you," Shark explained. "This isn't over until I say it's over!"

He then threatened them as his voice changed to a bloody murderous tone.

"Now if you two worthless chunks of crap think you want to try and stop me, I will crucify you both," Shark yelled. "UNDERSTOOD?!"

The frightened Hamilton Brothers whimpered, "Y...Y...Yes, sir."

Shark replied calmly, "Good boys."

Shark explained his evil plan to the Hamilton Brothers. I'll explain it more fully in a few more pages. Right now I'll let Shark do his evil speech of evil.

"Now, I'll once again explain why I'm the only living being in existence that is God's chosen one," Shark claims. "The world is a dangerous place and I'm destined to fix it. When I first laid my eyes on Samantha, I realized I had been given an opportunity to make the new Son of God. That is until a *retard* ruined that chance, but that's all going to change tonight!"

It concerned Victor and Billy so much that they decided to go against this, "No."

Shark turned around in shock, "No?"

"No, this is seriously messed up, man," Victor replied. "We realized that Sammy is a very nice girl. Trying to spy on Sammy is one thing, but trying to torture her? This is going way too far!"

"Yeah," Billy nodded. "what he says, Shark! I wanna go home!!"

"Besides, Mr. Poo-poo head," Victor mocked Shark. "Why can't you just go home to your Mommy and Daddy and lay an egg?"

The boys were laughing which causes Shark to angrily grab Victor by the shirt and point a gun at his chin, much to Billy's horror. "ENOUGH!" Shark barked as he pulled Victor close to him. "You two have no idea who you're talking to and if either of you mention my mother and father again, I'll blow both of your heads off!" Shark glared right between the eyes at Victor. 'gulp'

"Besides, this is an act of God, and we are stuck to it. You cannot pull away," Shark explained. "And when Christmas has passed and our deed is done, the new Son of God will be born. I can sense it." This information frightened the Hamilton Brothers, but this time, they sadly decided to go with it.

"S...S...Sure, man," Victor said as Billy nodded. "B..."

"BUT WHAT?!" Shark chimed in.

"But what about Hopkins?" Victor whimpered.

Shark replied evilly, "Leave him to me."

****

After we left the Teammates, we walked Sammy and Mikey back home. Sammy gave me my jacket back. Sammy explained that she is finally getting a new job as a therapist she's always wanted and she won't be my community habilitation worker anymore.

We both agreed that even though she may not work for me anymore, we can still be friends. I'm not sure she realizes I have feelings for her. Sammy thanked me for letting her use my jacket. We were unsure if we should kiss each other good night. Besides she is my community habilitation worker, well at least for now.

"I had a good time, Shorty. Thank you." Sammy said.

"You're welcome, Sammy." I replied. "We'll have to do it again sometime."

"Absolutely." Sammy replied.

Mom, Stephanie, Butchie and I said good-night to Sammy and Mikey outside their apartment building. Sammy and Mikey walked into the lobby. Much to her shock, Shark and the Hamilton Brothers were waiting for her in a dark corner. Like I said before, the guy never quits with his disturbing surprises.

"Hey sweetie," Shark said evilly, "Home so soon?"

Startled, Sammy responded, "Shark?" She ordered Mikey to get behind her and groaned, "Why are you here, Shark?"

Shark said softly, "Well we haven't seen each other for a while so I thought we should spend some quality time together at my very own "Garden of Eden" for old time's sake."

Sammy tried to ignore him and walk away to the elevator. Shark grabbed Mikey and pointed a gun at him, which terrified Sammy and the Hamilton Brothers. She couldn't believe Shark would have the guts to kill an innocent child. Shark blackmailed Sammy that if she doesn't come with him right now, he will send Mikey to eternal life.

"So sad to see an unfortunate soul die at a young age, isn't it, Samantha," Shark said sadistically. "So what's it going to be?"

With no other way out, Sammy surrendered herself and sadly sighed, "You win."

Shark smiled, "Excellent."

Victor and Billy looked at each other. They were impressed with Sammy's sacrifice.

Sammy cried, "Just promise me you'll let him go, please."

Shark chuckled, "Anything for my sweetheart."

Shark released Mikey who ran towards Sammy and they hugged. Momentarily, Victor and Billy were both touched by their affection. Shark impatiently points and cocks a gun at Sammy's head.

"Enough of this nonsense!" Shark shouted. "Now tell your squirt to leave this moment."

"Leave now, Mikey," Sammy whispered. "Don't look back."

Mikey ran towards the elevator in fear while Sammy stood up.

"Samantha Johnson," Shark said as he handcuffed her, "you are under arrest."

She ordered Shark to let her go. Shark slapped her, much to Victor and Billy's horror.

"No way, sweet cheeks," Shark said. "I'm taking you for a ride. Besides, you don't need to keep living with an old bag yeti of a grandmother now do you?"

Shark pointed the gun and ordered the Hamilton Brothers to help him put Sammy in the trunk of his carjacked convertible. He drove away as she was screaming for help inside. She sounded scared and terrified. Victor and Billy felt guilty for letting Shark kidnap Sammy.

****

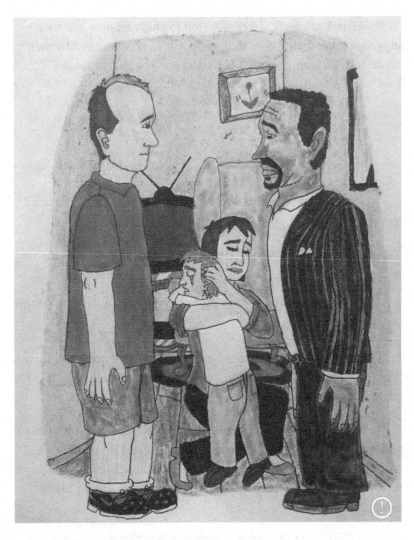

The next day, it was Christmas Eve and I was getting excited for Christmas the next day. Everybody else, however, was concerned about Sammy's disappearance. I'm concerned for Sammy too, but I am still excited about Christmas.

Mom wanted to support Sammy's family over the crazy situation. I could use some support myself. Seriously, how many loved ones do I have to lose right now? I mean what did I ever do to deserve this?

When Mom and I went to Sammy's apartment, some other people arrived before us. Mikey was upset that Sammy's gone. He was crying and said, "I wish I could have helped her. She's with that crazy guy." Mom comforted him by hugging him.

"Oh, Mikey, we're so sorry," Mom said.

"Where is she?" Mikey cried. "Where is my sister? I don't know how to live without her."

"Oh I know, Mikey," Mom said as she hugged him. "I know."

As Mom and Mikey were having a scene here, I walked around the apartment until I bumped into someone Sammy knew. "Sorry."

Jerome said, "You must be Shorty."

I replied, "Yes, sir."

Jerome introduced himself, "My name is Jerome Myllek and I'm Sammy's manager at CVS."

"Oh, nice to meet you, sir." I replied as we shook hands. "Sammy thinks of you like a father."

Jerome explained, "Sammy told me a lot about you."

"Really?" I asked.

"Yes," Jerome replied. "Sammy said that you were very supportive to her and she appreciated that."

"Wow!" I said. "Strong words."

"She also said that if it wasn't for you," Jerome continued. "she would never have confidence in anybody. I want to thank you for that."

"You're welcome." I replied in a melancholy tone.

While I continued walking around the apartment, I saw Joan in Sammy's room. She was so devastated by her loss and blamed me because she thought I was somehow responsible for her disappearance.

"I just know it's your fault she's gone!" Joan shouted. "I blame you, Shorty Hopkins! You...you..."

"What?" I said. "But I have nothing to do with..."

Mom thinks it's better if we leave.

"Go to hell, Shorty!" Joan growls. "YOU'RE A DEVIL! YOU'RE A DEVIL! YOU'RE A DEVIL!"

Mom hates the way people bad mouth me, but she knows that Joan is already having a difficult time right now.

"Oh she doesn't mean it, sweetheart," Mom explained. "Joan is very upset over Sammy's disappearance."

****

At my apartment, Butchie and Stephanie were sitting on the couch together, watching their favorite movie. When their favorite song was played during the end of the movie, they were dancing along.

"You can do it, Butchie," Stephanie said as she dances.

"Yep," Butchie replied.

As they continued, Old Man Edward shouted underneath the floor, "WILL YOU PLEASE STOP THAT EARTHQUAKE!!!!"

"Oh shut up, Old Man Edward!" Stephanie shouted back.

"Yeah," Butchie chimed in. "Shut up!"

They gave each other a high five and continued dancing to their catchy tune.

When the song was over, they got back to the couch. Mom and I came through the door. Mom was concerned about Joan. "I realize her grandmother is very upset, but that woman acts as though you killed Sammy or something."

"What?!" I asked loudly. "Don't think she's dead."

Shocked at my current statement, Mom angrily responded, "Shorty Hopkins, That is a stupid thing to say."

I tried to explain that I only just said that out of my concern for Sammy, not out of stupidity. But Mom doesn't think so. Mom thinks that I don't think of anybody but myself.

"Think before you say anything. I think your autism is getting in the way!"

Once again, I tried to explain something, but I decided not to try to convince her. "Aw forget it," I responded. "You don't even understand me anyway! That's the problem!"

"Oh No! No! No! No! No!" Mom shouted. "The only problem is that sometimes you've been such a pain! Not everything is about your father and death!"

"How dare you say that about my father!" I replied. "This has nothing to do with him."

Mom yelled that I'm annoying, controlling, and that she dislikes my current attitude.

I interrupted Mom. "Oh there you go with your constant nagging again!"

In return, Mom then repeats that I'm the most annoying person she knows.

I said, "I'm annoying?"

"Yes, Shorty!" Mom replied. "You are!"

"You always criticize my behavior," I complained. "Well you don't have every right to control me, you...you...you're always nagging at me!"

Shocked by my harsh statement, Mom angrily left the room as I headed towards my bedroom. "Well I can't argue with that! I'm leaving, you CRAZY LUNATIC!" Mom yelled, "I'm not fighting with you! And I'm not talking to you WHEN YOU'RE MAKING NO SENSE!"

I angrily responded as she exited the apartment door, "FINE, DON'T HURRY BACK!"

We both slammed our doors. Butchie and Stephanie overheard my heated argument with my mother. They looked at each other and were both wondering what to do about it.

I was sitting on my bed, thinking, demoralized by the recent events and I started to realize that Mom is right about me. I really do think only about myself. As I looked out the window, my anger melted into sadness. My eyes watered and I collapsed onto my bed, silently crying into my arms.

To be honest, no matter what happens, I just want to show some positive emotions. I'm starting to realize that I love Sammy and I feel so selfish to realize that. I'm sadly beginning to lose hope.

Suddenly, there was a knock on the door. Instead of answering the door like I usually do, I decided to let the visitor in, "Come in."

The door opened. It was Butchie and Stephanie.

"You okay, buddy?" Butchie asked.

"Yeah, Shorty," Stephanie chimed in. "You got to pull yourself together."

"What's the point, guys?" I replied in despair. "I mean I do love Sammy, but she disappeared and I was too stupid to see that. I mean Mom is right, Dad was right and everybody is right. I do think about myself. I wish I could show people I do think of others, but I think it's too late to change that."

They told me that they overheard my heated argument with Mom. They came to encourage me to rescue Sammy.

"Listen, Shorty," Stephanie explained. "It's never too late. Let's find Sammy and prove you can think of someone besides yourself,"

Butchie chimed in, "Yeah buddy."

"Besides," Stephanie continued. "You should never give up no matter what and there will be some good days and some dark days ahead of us. There will be days where you feel all alone and that's when it's the most difficult to keep hope alive."

Butchie nodded with her.

I realized that they're right. Even though I might get grounded for sneaking out of the apartment, but this was my chance to be a hero the same way they do in the movies. I left a big note for Mom so she wouldn't be confused. We left home to go save the day. I feel like I'm becoming a superhero rescuing a damsel in distress like when Clark Kent changed into Superman in order to save Lois Lane and when Peter Parker changed into Spider-Man in order to save Mary Jane Watson. Pretty exciting, isn't it?

Besides, like what Spider-Man learned from his late uncle, father figure and influence, Ben Parker: "With Great Power, Comes Great Responsibility."

I saw it in a movie once. It really helped grief-stricken people who lost their loved ones and the moral message of the death scene and the ending really speaks to me.

****

Warning

The scene you are about to read contains material not suitable for younger readers. The illustration might be disturbing to some readers

Reader discretion is advised.

Meanwhile in the abandoned building at the "Garden of Eden," Shark had a thousand candles all over his "Garden of Eden" room like in that horror movie, Carrie (1976), which I find pretty creepy.

Shark, who had gone completely insane, had Sammy all tied up to his bed in the "Garden of Eden," making her feel like an object. He had made Sammy dress differently in the "present" he had "given" her. He gave her a very short, revealing pink dress to wear, something Sammy never would have worn unless she was forced.

He ordered the Hamilton Brothers to burn Sammy's red dress. Victor secretly kept the dress, as he doesn't want "a perfectly good dress to go to waste." Victor hid the dress. Billy doesn't know where it is.

Sammy vulnerably looks up to Shark in fear, her heart thudding in her chest. Shark's eyes fixed on Sammy's and there is a crazed awful passion in them. He put the same diamond necklace he stole around her neck.

"Merry Christmas, my love," Shark said with a creepy smirk on his face. "I hope you like it."

Sammy tearfully nodded as Shark asked her, "Do you know why I'm God's perfect child, Samantha?" Sammy shook her head in fear.

"I'm God's perfect child because while the world is a very sinful place, I always follow the Bible, trying to bring peace and harmony by fixing all the mistakes God made." Shark explained, "You are my Eve, Samantha. We're not whole without the other. Since God made us, it's our destiny to become one and to create a new life in the image of God. One day, you will bear my child." This comment horrified Sammy and the Hamilton Brothers.

"No! It's not true," Sammy cried out. "It can't be true!"

"Oh you know in your heart it is, my Mary," Shark responded as he chuckled. "God wanted us to be the next Mary and Joseph and have our very own Jesus. When he grows a little older, we will teach him about the real meaning of "peace and harmony" and bring a new and better world by fixing all of God's mistakes. A world with no retards* and cripples."

His view of "peace and harmony" and "better world" is exterminating disabled people, not curing or helping them. This information really disturbed Sammy and the Hamilton Brothers.

Shark saw Sammy as she sadly bent her head down and asked, "What's the matter, Sweetheart? You're not having a good time with me tonight?"

Sammy went emotionally silent. Shark slapped her really hard. "You're still thinking about that fat potato-headed *retard*, aren't you?! AREN'T YOU?!" Shark shouted. "Well maybe I'll kill him if you don't do as I say." He pointed a gun at her.

Sammy was frightened, and begged him not to do this. Shark responded disturbingly, "Shhh! It's okay, Honey. I'm here. I'm here."

He also forced a frightened Sammy to announce her "love" for him by pointing a gun at her forehead. "CONFESS YOUR LOVE, NOW!!!" Shark yelled as Sammy whimpered, "I love you, Shark," she said, her voice quivering in fear. "I love you."

Shark stopped when he saw the Hamilton Brothers standing there, watching and whispering to each other.

Victor whispered, "Man, he has serious issues."

Billy responded, "Tell me about it."

Shark yelled as he got off his bed, "What are you two idiots still doing here? GET LOST!!!!"

Quivering and shocked, Victor complained, "But, Shark. You promised us that if we help you, we would get a reward."

Billy responded, "Yeah!"

Shark angrily yelled, "Ha! You're both nothing to me. I lied about the reward. There never was a reward. I only wanted to get my Eve back and I used you like the pathetic losers you are. So you two feeble-minded morons shut your mouths and SCRAM!!!!!"

Victor and Billy were shocked that Shark betrayed them. They sadly left and Sammy was hoping they would go get help for her. She feels bad for them that they got mixed up with Shark, but how could they have let this craziness go on so long? Didn't they see that the "Garden of Eden" is part of Shark's insanity? Sammy hopes and prays they finally do the right thing and get her some help.

"*Damn*! I'm smooth. I used those two guys for my own purposes," Shark said with a grin.

Shark went back to Sammy without a second thought about the Hamilton Brothers. "Now where were we?"

Sammy angrily yelled, "DROP DEAD!!"

Shark roughly grabbed her by the neck, "Don't you ever say that to me again! ARE WE CLEAR?!"

Sammy nodded as she was choking. He let go of her neck. "Good girl."

Shark continued to interrogate Sammy about me. "So how long have you known Hopkins?"

Sammy responded, "It's none of your business!"

Shark brutally slapped her again. "I told you to never yell at me like that again!"

"Now I don't want you to see that disabled freak again!" Shark continued. "ARE WE ONCE AGAIN CLEAR?!!"

Sammy looked down in defeat and tearfully said, "Yes."

"Good girl," Shark menacingly commented. "Now you still love me, don't you?"

Sammy said nothing until Shark pointed his gun and cocked it.

Sammy nodded as he demanded, "Well then, once again, confess your love for me."

Sammy whimpered, "I love you."

Shark asked her as he placed his ear near her mouth, "What was that?"

Sammy once again whimpered, "I love you."

Shark kissed her, which made Sammy feel very uncomfortable.

"Oh my love," Shark said with a grin as he sniffed her hair and touched her inner thigh. "God surely smiled on you, didn't he?" He is really amazed how soft her skin is.

Sammy cried, "No, get away from me."

"Oh don't ruin our union, Samantha," Shark responded "calmly". "God has been looking forward to bless this day since the crucifixion of Jesus."

"Since then, God thinks there should be a new magical baby," Shark stated. "He finds you to be the next mother of the new Son of God, Samantha, and since I'm God's perfect child, He gave me a magic seed to plant the new and improved Jesus Christ!!"

"You're not a Christian," Sammy yelled. "You're a sick monster!!!!"

Once again, he grabbed her by the neck, "What did I say about calling me names?"

Sammy frighteningly apologized, "Sorry."

Shark replied, "That's more like it."

Shark decided to head out for a few minutes, "I'm going to get a few things and pray for our union. Maybe when I get back, we should have a little "fun" tonight."

"I'm looking forward to it," Sammy said as she pretended to be excited for his affection, smiling at him, although she was scared inside.

"That's more like it." Shark said with a smirk on his face as he blew a kiss to her and walked out the door.

While she was still tied to the bed, Sammy emotionally lost all hope and realized her fate. She was afraid she was going to be raped by Shark and started to cry even harder. She said to herself tearfully, "I'm sorry, Shorty."

Author's note: Remember kids, teenagers and adults, you have to be careful about talking to strangers.

There are disturbed people out there that will take advantage of you.

****

After Mom and I argued, she went to Diane's apartment to pull herself together before she exploded. While there, Diane listened to Mom's complaints that I'm the most egotistical and insufferable person she has ever met.

Diane responded, "Don't feel that way, Betty."

Mom then announces that she can't live with me for another minute. It concerned Diane.

Diane asked, "Why are you giving up?"

Mom replied, "I'm not giving up."

"You are," Diane said. "You're giving up on your own son."

"But he's 25 years old," Mom sighed. "He's always trying to be a smart ass and I don't know why. I just... I can't get through to him anymore. It used to be that I'd be able to easily know what he was thinking. But the last year or so...I just don't know. Every time I try to change one thing in his God forsaken room, he has a temper tantrum. Holy cow does my head hurt!!" Betty grabbed her head in pain for a second.

"There you go again, cutting yourself short, Betty," Diane said. "You act like Shorty is always in charge of you. Well guess what, he's not. Betty, you're sweet, funny and smart. You are strong and have done an amazing job raising Shorty. You've always been a good mother to him no matter what," Diane told Betty.

"You're absolutely right, Diane," Betty said. "Maybe I can just talk to Shorty softly about his behavior; we won't have to get into another argument."

Diane always gives Mom parenting advice about how she could interact with me better no matter what the situations are. Really cool, huh? Anyway, Mom came back home from Diane's apartment next door. She sighed as she entered the door.

"Shorty, we need to talk. I...Shorty?" Mom said as she realized that I'm not here and spotted a note on my bedroom door. The note said,

"Dear Mom.

I went to rescue Sammy. Butchie and Stephanie are with me. Don't worry. I'll be back. I know I'm probably going to get grounded for this. In case anything happens to me, I just want to say I'm sorry. You're an awesome mother. You raised me by example and time after time, I've seen you put other people's needs first. I can't obey you now without disobeying everything you've ever taught me about life, the world, and responsibility.

Love,
Shorty Hopkins"

When Mom finished reading it, she said, "Oh no!"

She was worried for our safety and rushed out the door and went next door to Diane's apartment. She knocked on the door.

As Diane opened it, Mom explained, "They're gone!"

Diane responded, "And so is Stephanie."

Mom pointed out that she read a note and they should go in search of us before we get hurt or killed.

As they were waiting in the elevator, Victor and Billy's parents, who lived a floor below, got in the elevator and were arguing loudly. Each blamed the other for losing the boys. Mom finally had it with the argument and yelled at both of them. She pointed out that it's both side's fault that their boys are lost. She told them they have been so focused on insults, grudges, and even years worth of minor fights and disagreements that they forgot about the most important thing in their lives: their children. Mom also said, "Diane and I are going in search of our children. I hope your boys did not have anything to do with their disappearance."

Finally remorseful over what they've done, the Hamilton parents decide to work together to help Mom and Diane to find us. Their boys had not come home yet and they were hoping they had nothing to do with the children missing.

****

Butchie, Stephanie and I left our apartment to go find Sammy. I gotta tell ya, it's like a big life-changing adventure like they do in the movies.

I also feel like I'm in the Wizard of Oz, except I'm not some girl from Kansas who traveled to a magical land with her beloved dog following the yellow brick road, and there's no scarecrow who seeks a brain, a tin man who seeks a heart and a cowardly lion who seeks some courage, singing along about our journey while being tracked-down by an evil and vengeful witch until there is no place like home.

We went to Maureen and Caitlin's apartment. We explained to them what we were doing. They agreed to help. Maureen brought her karate gear which concerned Caitlin. She wanted Maureen to put the gear down. Maureen gave in, even though she thought a weapon might be necessary. Caitlin was really happy that Maureen got some sense and left her karate gear behind.

We went to Sammy's apartment. Mikey was home alone and was very worried about his sister's disappearance. His grandmother had gone to the police station to see if they could help find Sammy. We explained that we're going to rescue Sammy. At first, Mikey was worried that he might get in trouble, but I explained that Sammy is counting on us. He decided to join in.

"I'm in," Mikey said.

After we got Mikey, I decided it would be best if we got more people to help us. We decided to go to Angie's place.

She and Peter Dreggs were at their fancy garden house, wearing their Ancient Roman outfits. There is fancy French music. Their artist is painting a portrait of them making a weird pose until we arrived.

Dreggs asked, "What are YOU doing here, Hopkins? You're disrupting our peace."

Angie agreed, "Yeah."

"There's no time for insults, guys," I explained. "Sammy is in trouble and we need your help."

Angie and Dreggs are confused that their rival wants their help.

"Look," I responded. "I know it sounds crazy, guys, but we have to keep our friends close and enemies closer. So we have to save her. Let's go."

"Very well, Hopkins," Dreggs replied. "We'll go along with your little nonsense for now, but after this, the change is... Nothing."

"Precisely, Petey-dear," Angie chimed in. "Precisely."

Stephanie, Butchie and I looked at each other awkwardly and Maureen and Caitlin looked really annoyed with Dreggs and Angie's rudeness. Mikey thinks they're funny since he's giggling about their outfits.

As we all left, the artist was standing with his art unfinished. There was a quiet wind sound blowing, whistling, but nothing blew away. The artist was all alone and asked, "Can I at least use the restroom?"

****

Meanwhile, Mom, Diane and the Hamilton parents had gone to the police station because they figured it would be best if the police helped find us.

Mom tried to explain to the police captain about their children's disappearance. She wasn't sure where we had gone, but Shark might have kidnapped Sammy and we all could be in danger.

Captain Oliver explained, "The police are doing everything we can to find Shark. You know he killed two of our police officers. Everyone else should let the police do our job and not interfere."

Mom complained, "You don't understand, Captain! Shark is a psycho and he will kill my son! We need to find my son, Shorty, before he finds Shark and gets himself killed."

Captain Oliver said, "We're on it, ma'am." Exasperated, Mom, Diane and the Hamilton parents turned away from the desk to leave the police station.

Suddenly, Joan arrived at the police station. She still blamed me, believing that I'm guilty. Joan thought I was involved with Sammy's disappearance and said to Captain Oliver that Sammy would be better off if I was put in prison.

Mom furiously replied, "How dare you blame my son for your granddaughter's disappearance! Shorty did nothing to her! Sammy was just trying to help him get out more! Now we're going to find our children. I suggest if you want to see Sammy again, you will stop bad mouthing my son and you will HELP US!!"

Realizing that Mom was right, Joan responded as she tagged along. "Wait!! I'll join you!"

While they were searching throughout the neighborhood for their children, Mom told Joan every single thing Sammy and I had done together.

"Look, Joan," Mom explained. "Shorty may not be perfect, but he's done a lot of good things with Sammy and everybody else."

With Mom's words, Joan ultimately is starting to regret bad mouthing me.

****

Meanwhile outside Shark's building, the devastated Victor and Billy felt betrayed. Billy was really upset while Victor was really mad about Shark being such a jerk. He tipped the garbage cans outside out of anger.

"That jerk," Victor shouted. "That big fat dumb jerk! He duped us! He planned it all along and we fell for it!" Billy cried as Victor comforted him.

Suddenly, they saw us walking. Victor thought that they should help us find Sammy.

Billy was concerned about this at first, but Victor stated, "Look, Billy. Shark LIED to us and he used us to get what he wanted. So I think it is time for us to stop following Shark's orders and start doing the right thing or else we can get into big trouble for helping Shark."

Billy finally realized that Victor was right, as much as he hated to admit it, "I can't believe I'm saying this, but you're right, man!"

"Of course I am." Victor said as Billy smiled. "Now come on."

Meanwhile, we were all doubting where Sammy's location was until the Hamilton Brothers shows up.

"Hey everybody!" Victor shouted excitedly. "The back-up has arrived."

"Yeah." Billy echoed in an exhausted voice. "God, I need some water. Does anybody have water?"

"Not now, Pea-brain!" Victor shouted.

Frightened, Mikey hid right behind me. At first, I didn't trust them at first because they worked for Shark.

Even though I really could not trust them, I asked, "What brings you two here?"

"I...uh...I know some stuff that could be helpful." Victor replied nervously.

"Helpful?" I asked. "How?"

"We know where Sammy is." Victor explained as Billy nodded.

"Why should we believe you two jerks?" Maureen shouted.

Caitlin glared. "Maureen!"

Insulted, Billy shouted. "Hey, who are you calling a jerk, jerk?"

"Billy!" Victor said. "Now is not the time!"

"Look, no offense, guys." I was still unsure of them. "But I think it's difficult for us to believe that you two are helping us."

"Now wait a minute, Shorty!" Mikey replied. "I think we should listen to what these guys have to say."

Everybody was confused, "Huh?"

"One time, Sammy says that it's important to forgive and forget." Mikey explained. "Move forward instead of looking back."

Everybody agreed with him, including myself. "Strong words, kiddo," I said as I patted his head and messed his hair. "Alright, guys. We're all ears."

"Okay." Victor explained. "Right before Shark betrayed and kicked us out..."

"He's a big meanie!!" Billy cried.

"As I was saying," Victor continued. "We saw Sammy getting tortured by that monster. It really scared us. What Shark is planning to do to her is completely insane. He wants to make a new Jesus or something."

As they explained, I asked, "What are you guys talking about…?" I suddenly stopped myself and remembered what my father taught me long ago, "Oh no." I said.

"What's wrong, Shorty?" Stephanie asked.

"I think I know what these guys are talking about." I said.

"What's that, pal?" Butchie asked.

"My father warned me about the dangers of what Shark's former minions are talking about," I explained. "What a really awful thing to do! If someone says "No" it means "NO.""

Maureen was shocked and became enraged when she hears what Shark plans on doing to Sammy and shouted, "WHY THAT EVIL SON OF A…!"

"Easy, Maureen." Caitlin chimed in as she put her hand on her shoulder. Maureen calms down.

"We're sorry." Victor said.

"Yeah." Billy said. "We didn't know Shark would do something so evil to Sammy."

"We know." I let them join us to rescue her from Shark. "So where is Sammy?"

Victor and Billy pointed in the direction of Shark's evil lair, the "Garden of Eden."

Mikey doesn't know what we were talking about and asked, "What are you guys talking about?"

"That's something you'll understand when you're older, kid." I responded, again messing his hair.

We entered the building as Shark returned to the candlelit room. He finished reading what he found inspiring. He believed what was said in *Deuteronomy 22:28-29* and *Leviticus 24:15-16* - A Blasphemer Put to Death:

"28 If a man happens to a berg in who is not pledged to be married and rapes her and they are discovered, 29 he shall pay her father fifty shekels of silver. He must marry the young woman, for he has violated her. He can never divorce her as long as he lives."

"15 Say to the Israelites: 'Anyone who curses their God will he held responsible; 16 anyone who blasphemes the name of the Lord is to be put to death. The entire assembly must stone them. Whether foreigner or native-born, when they blaspheme the Name they are to be put to death."

He prepared to have some "fun" with Sammy. He was mumbling that he thinks I am an imbecile and can't love her like she deserves. He sees Sammy as a weak little girl and he feels a sense of power having her still tied on his bed.

Sammy cried, "Please don't do this."

Shark approached Sammy with a creepy smirk on his face, "Well, Babe. The time has come for God to bless this union." Shark said as he was taking his belt off, "Like what it said in **Genesis 3:13'** *"And the Lord God said unto the woman, What is this that thou hast done? And the woman said, The serpent beguiled me, and I did eat."* So let's get it on."

Suddenly as Shark was about to take her top off, he and Sammy heard a door opening from downstairs. Shark ordered Sammy to stay there as he left the room.

We entered the building and the Hamilton Brothers told us Sammy was in the room directly upstairs. Shark saw us entering his evil lair. He decided to give us a big surprise.

The building was old, wrecked and deserted. Walking through there felt like some kind of a horror movie. It was dark and musty, and there were spider webs that needed to be cleared away in order to walk up the stairs. Angie and Peter were disgusted and they ran off like the cowards they are.

As we were about to walk upstairs, I felt I should do this by myself. I've already lost my father and I was afraid I might lose my best friends through all this.

"You know what, guys?" I said nervously. "I think I should do this by myself."

"But Shorty," Stephanie said. "We're in this together."

"Yeah," Butchie responded. "we're your best friends, buddy."

I fully explained to everyone why I should handle Shark by myself.

"I know, guys," I explained. "But I'm afraid that if you guys face Shark with me, I might lose you like I lost my father. So this is for your own good."

"Whatever you say, man." Butchie replied.

"Okay, Shorty," Stephanie said. "We understand, but be careful."

I smiled and hugged them both.

I went upstairs. The Hamilton Brothers decided to run off like the cowards they are.

"Well, he's a dead man," Billy stated. "We tried. Let's go."

"Yeah," Victor stated. "Adios. It was good to see you guys."

Angered, Maureen grabbed the Hamilton Brothers by their shirts and shoved them against the wall.

"We do not play games," Maureen shouted. "Now either you two *damn* fools are going to help us or I'll bust your sorry *asses*! UNDERSTAND?!!!!"

Whimpering, The Hamilton Brothers cowardly nodded, "Yes, ma'am."

The police arrived. Officer John Wall and Officer Paulie Martino, a couple of old friends of my father's, showed up and ordered the rest of the kids to leave for their own safety except for Victor and Billy.

John and Paulie interrogated the Hamilton Brothers since they worked for Shark.

"Alright, punks," Officer John shouted as Paulie nodded. "Where are Shark, Shorty and Sammy?"

They explained that I had gone ahead to look for Sammy. They told them that they're not with Shark anymore and what Shark's evil plan is.

"Really?" Officer John said as he acted like he's not falling for their story, "Well why don't we go check?"

Victor and Billy looked at each other and nodded.

****

While I was walking through the hallways to look for Sammy, I noticed Shark wrote some words and numbers in blood, which I found really disturbing. "Crud." I said quietly.

Sammy heard footsteps and she got scared because she thought it was Shark's footsteps. She thought Shark was coming back.

As I entered the "Garden of Eden" room, I was thrilled to see her, but Sammy refused my rescue because if Shark saw us here, he would kill us. As I was untying her from the bed, I tried to convince her that I came here to rescue her.

"No, Shorty," Sammy whispered. "You must go before he gets back and finds you."

"No, Sammy," I whispered. "I'm not leaving without you."

Shark appeared. "Samantha's right, Hopkins. You shouldn't have come here."

Sammy and I were both horrified to see him. "Oh my God." I said. "Shark!"

Shark said evilly, "It's so good to see you again."

I responded sarcastically, "Can't say the same for you, murderer!"

"I'm not a murderer, Hopkins. I'm just a Christian who is helping God fix his mistakes."

"You're not a Christian, Shark, You're a monster!" I angrily responded. "How dare you kill those police officers? What would your parents think of this?!"

"You leave mother and father out of this!" Shark yelled, as he wanted to forget his own relation with his parents and pretend it never even existed since they showed him selfishness and neglect. "They gave me misery and shame. They deserved to suffer!! THIS WORLD DESERVES TO SUFFER!!!!"

During my confrontation with Shark, Sammy wanted to make it less difficult. She said, "Shorty, it's impossible to reason with him." I was just trying to help Shark see how wrong he was, even though he's one of those people who can't just wake up, realize the error of their ways, and clean up the mess he made.

"Look, I know what they did to you was wrong, but that doesn't mean they deserved to die!!" I explained.

As I tried to continue, Shark got annoyed with my statement. "This is your greatest weakness, isn't it, Hopkins?" Shark laughed. "Your attachment, love, and compassion for others. Well guess what? They're all nothing but an illusion, a lie, a fake, a weakness, and a disgrace."

"Man!" I asked. "Don't you think of anybody or anything but yourself, Shark?"

"Unlike you and Samantha," Shark explained. "I have the discipline of mind to not be bogged down by any petty emotions."

"You are seriously messed up, Shark!" I responded. "I mean for real!"

Shark began taunting me for loving Sammy, "Do you love her, Hopkins?" Shark asked sadistically, "Do you honestly think that she would want to be with a *retard* like you?"

"Shut up!" I yelled. "You shut up and keep your filthy hands off of her!"

He mocked, "You better watch your mouth, Hopkins, or you'll end up dead, just like your father."

"What?!" I asked. "How do you know about my father? He died from cancer years ago."

Shark said that he believed when my father was in the hospital, he was killed by a highly toxic poison. "As your father, he was one of God's mistakes," Shark said. "Whoever injected him was doing God a favor."

He took great delight in telling me this and I angrily yelled, "That's a lie!"

"Is it?" Shark chuckled sadistically. "Well let me tell you something about what's wrong with this world, Hopkins. It's always trying to make people perfect. But unfortunately, it can't. People like you don't fit in this world. You're all just God's ultimate mistakes."

I felt like I wanted to whack the guy's teeth out of his mouth as my fists are shaking.

"Face it, Hopkins, you and your *retard* friends and family have no right to claim to speak for severely autistic people who can't speak for themselves. You're not perfect. I am the only one who is perfect because...I'M GOD'S PERFECT CHILD!"

That was the most offensive thing anybody has ever said to my friends and me. I angrily approached Shark as I grumbled and explained what my parents taught me about the real meaning of being disabled. "You're wrong, Shark. Disabled people are not God's mistakes." As I was going on with my speech, Shark was becoming infuriated by this while Sammy was impressed. "Just because we're different doesn't mean it's a bad thing. I've seen a lot of disabled people doing great things for the world. And year after year, people are inspired by people with autism. There are artists, scientists, doctors, magicians, poets, and actors who happen to have autism. You should just travel around the world and see. There's also non disabled people like Sammy here and she felt good helping people who are disabled, including myself. No matter what happens, inspiration is everywhere! So who's God's mistake now, huh? We're all perfect no matter what. God made us who we are and that's OK by me!! If you don't like it, THAT'S YOUR PROBLEM!!! I mean for what you have done in your life, there's a place in *hell* for someone like you. Besides, our whole lives are like pieces of a puzzle. We try to put things together mentally and you know that, don't you?"

Enraged, Shark slapped me in the face with his gun and I fell to the ground, much to Sammy's horror. "Pretty words for a ***RETARD!***" Shark responded as he grabbed Sammy by the arm and pointed a gun at me. "You shouldn't have said that to me," Shark said. "I guess sometimes a retard* like you have to learn things the hard way."

"Let her go, Shark!" I shouted after I got off the ground. "This is between you and me!"

"Why should I?" Shark replied evilly. "I'm showing you what happens when you show your insolence."

Shark was pointing his gun at Sammy's head as he said to Sammy, ***"The house of the wicked will be destroyed, But the tent of the upright will flourish,"*** quoting **Proverbs 14:11**

"No, Shark!" I shouted. "Please just take me instead, I'll do anything you want!"

"Well isn't that romantic," Shark mocked. "A *retard* plans to go to hell for all eternity for his precious angel, correct?"

"Yes," I sadly nodded. "Just don't hurt her, Okay?"

"You fool!!" Shark mocked again. "Why should I choose? I can do anything I want. I can kill you and have her."

I gotta tell ya. The way he said that, it shows how totally ruthless he is.

"Now," Shark demands. "kneel before me or else your lover dies."

I just stood there daydreaming for a second until Shark cocked the gun to shoot Sammy in the head, "Stop!" I yelled. "I'll do it."

As I kneeled, Sammy tried to stop me, as she screamed, "NO, SHORTY!! DON'T DO IT!!"

I responded, "It's okay, Sammy."

Sammy cried, "JUST GET OUT OF HERE!!"

"SHUT UP, WITCH!!" Shark yelled. "YOU DON'T GET TO DECIDE, I DO!!"

The frightened Sammy apologized, "Sorry."

As he pointed the pistol at me Shark asked me, "Any last words before I sentence you to *hell*, Hopkins?"

I sadly confessed, "Yes."

I turned to Sammy, "Sammy, tell my Mom that she gave me a wonderful life and I'm eternally grateful that she brought me into this world and for being my mother." Sammy was touched while Shark rolled his eyes.

I concluded, "And one last thing I need to say."

Sammy nodded in response.

"I...I...I love you, Sammy." I said as a tear brimmed and fell from my eye.

Sammy sadly responded as Shark impatiently sighed, "I love you too, Shorty."

Shark chuckled and said, "Enough of this now. This might be the final speech you'll ever give. Those sure were pretty words of compassion for a *retard*."

"No Shorty," Sammy cried. "You don't know what you're doing!!!!!"

"I TOLD YOU TO SHUT UP!!" Shark shouted.

"Sorry." Sammy replied, tearfully, "Sorry."

"Now, you should have stayed out of this, Hopkins." Shark said, "But it's too late to change that."

"Yeah," I replied. "I should have. But no matter what happens, you can't have her!"

"I am tired of your insolence." Shark growled. "Goodbye, Hopkins. I hope you enjoy *hell*!!"

Instead of running off like a coward, I closed my eyes because I would rather die saving the woman I love than being a coward. I whispered, "W X Y Z." A gun fired.

Suddenly, I didn't feel anything. I opened my eyes and realized it wasn't Shark's trigger that was pulled. It was actually Shark who got shot and he dropped dead.

Officers John and Paulie, along with the Hamilton Brothers, showed up at just the right time.

"Actually, I was going to say the same thing about you, punk!" said Officer John.

"Yeah," Paulie replied "Now it would be a good time for you to shut up,"

"Oh my God!" Billy said amazed. "That was the definition of AWESOME!!!"

Victor responded, "Nice!!"

Officer John asked, "Are you kids alright?"

"Hey, like a famous band always said, I get by with a little help from my friends," We laughed together, as we all know what I mean. We could all feel the relief in the room.

"Sorry, that was from the Beatles," I said. "Right, Sammy?" Sammy replied as she tearfully gave me a big hug, "You got that right." She looked up at me. "You are a hero...my hero!"

Sammy and I reunited with a big hug. I rocked her and comforted her as she cried in my arms, "It's okay, Sammy," I said. "I'm here."

The Hamilton Brothers were smirking at each other when they saw us embracing.

We went over to Officers John and Paulie. We thanked them for saving our lives. "We're glad you guys are protecting us." I said, "We are so grateful."

"Well that's what we do." Officer John replied.

"Oh yeah!!" Billy said to Shark's corpse. "Who's a feeble minded moron now, LOSER?"

"OK, Billy," Victor said as he touched Billy on his shoulder. "That's enough."

Kids, I must warn you. Guys like Shark don't change. Do you think they ever suddenly wake up and realize their mistakes and clean up their act? No! They just keep ruining everyone's lives. It's sad to say that the world is better off without them. Don't let anger and rage go through your head or else you'll end up like Shark was: a conniving black-hearted monster.

I noticed Sammy's new outfit. I asked. "Where's your dress, Sammy?"

Sammy replied as Officer John and Paulie took the blanket off of Shark's bed and wrap it around her so no one would see anything if you know what I mean. "Shark had made me dress like this and forced the Hamilton Brothers to burn it."

Billy looks suspicious and Victor looks down with a guilty look. "I...I saved it, though," Victor said. "I hid the dress right over here." With that he walked out of the room and came back a moment later holding the dress and smiling. "It wasn't my size," he joked.

Billy shouted, "Dude, what the *hell*?! You don't wear no dresses!"

Victor replied, "I couldn't let a perfectly good dress go to waste."

"Too bad," Sammy said, smiling. "That color does look very nice on you though."

****

Both officers John and Paulie helped us get out of the building safely. We all reunited with our families, who were waiting outside in front with the police cars and the news reporters. There are sounds from the indistinct radio chatter. Angie and Peter, of course, weren't there because they ran off during the excitement like the cowards that they are.

Sammy gave the diamond necklace back to the police officer. "Thanks, ma'am. We were looking for that."

While Sammy was telling the officer the whole story about Shark, Mom ran up to me and hugged me so tightly.

She said, "Oh Shorty. Thank God you're alright."

I responded as I chuckled, "Okay, Mom. Okay."

Stephanie said, "Way to go, Shorty."

Butchie chimed in, "Yeah, Pal."

Mom asked me, "What were you doing in there?"

I explained that I rescued Sammy because I wanted to prove to her that I do think about others. "I don't know what I was thinking. I should have listened to you. I've been acting like a jerk lately and I'm sorry. I know you're just getting on my case because you're just looking after me."

Mom responded as she once again hugged me, "I am trying Sweetie and it's only because I love you."

I smiled and said, "I love you too, Mom." She also admitted that she is proud of me and understands what I needed to do.

Nearby, Sammy reunited with her friends and family. Mikey was so happy that his sister was all right. Joan burst into tears of joy while hugging Sammy.

"If anything happened to you," Joan cried. "I don't know what I would do."

Sammy responded, "I'm fine, Nana."

Joan said, "Listen, Sammy, um... I know I made a lot of mistakes with you. When you went missing, I cried like a baby and I was feeling sorry for myself like I was a bad parent."

Sammy tried to interrupt Joan, but Joan continued, "No listen, I know it's crazy for me to say this, but..."

Sammy was afraid that Joan was going to express her disapproval again. It surprised Sammy to hear her grandmother say, "I have to admit that I misjudged Shorty. He really is a decent fellow who cares a lot about you. I'm happy for both of you. I really am." She also explained, "I know that sometimes I could be pretty stubborn, but I'm just trying to figure out what's best for you."

Sammy tearfully replied, "I know, Nana."

Joan looked at the way Sammy was staring over at me while I was talking with my mother. "Tell me, Sammy." She asked, "Are you in love?"

Sammy nodded as she cried, "Yes, Nana. I think I am."

"His mother told me what you and Shorty have been doing and I'm proud that you're trying to help him," Joan explained as she started sobbing. "I know how much you love him. It's just...I don't know how to let you go."

They both hugged as they cried. Joan said, "I just want you to be happy, dear."

"I love you, Nana," Sammy replied. "I promise I'm not going anywhere for awhile." They both smiled.

This is interesting; Sammy and I are having touching moments with our mother and grandmother at the same time.

As I finished my moment with my mother, the Johnson family came towards me. Mikey thanked me for saving his big sister.

"Thanks, Shorty," Mikey said. "You're the best!"

"Sure thing, kiddo," I said as I gave him a high five. Mom thinks I'm acting like a cool guy.

"Look, Shorty." Joan confessed. "I know I've been tough on you. I didn't trust you with Sammy and you rescued her. I'm just afraid that I might lose my grandchildren like I lost their parents. I'm sorry. Let's just start over and if you would like to hang out with my granddaughter, then I guess that's okay with me."

I hugged her as I responded, "Thanks, Mrs. Johnson."

Joan stated, "Oh please, call me Joan."

Maureen and Caitlin also thanked me for saving their best friend.

"You sure got guts, fool." Maureen shouted.

Maureen's father Jerome had a ride to the crime scene and said, "Nice job, son."

"Yeah, Shorty," Caitlin agreed. "That was so brave of you."

"Thanks, girls," I nervously responded. "I'm just glad Officer John and Officer Paulie both showed up when they did."

After Sammy and I had our reunion with our loved ones, we turned our eyes on each other. It's like in the movie "West Side Story."

As we were about to kiss, Victor and Billy suddenly showed up. They also apologized to Sammy and me for working for Shark. We asked them why they were working for this guy. They explained their background. They were born in Goshen, Connecticut in 1963. After they moved to New York City as teenagers, they felt like big losers and did not know any people. The Hamilton Brothers met Shark sometime after Sammy broke up with Shark. When they first ran into Shark, he acted like he was lonely and he wanted some friends. That's why they hung out with him. They did not realize he wanted to surround himself with weak people that he could control.

"Besides," Victor said sympathetically. "All we ever wanted was a friend."

We accepted their apology because we knew they were just trying to be Shark's loyal friends. Even though they were trying to be good guys, their parents punished Victor and Billy. I was also surprised that their father is… Old Man Edward. I had never seen them altogether before!

"How many times do we have to tell you boys," Sharon yelled. "never talk to strangers?!"

The boys responded, bending their heads down, "Yes, Mommy."

Old Man Edward shouted as their mother pulled their ears, "You two whipper-snappers are in so much trouble." The boys screamed, "Ow! Ow! Ow! Ow! Ow! Ow!"

Mom called for us because we are going to the Teammates for Christmas Eve dinner. Sammy and I went with our friends and families.

Feeling bad for the Hamilton Brothers, Sammy explained to me that she thought we should repay them despite the fact that they worked for Shark. If it weren't for them, Shark's plan would have succeeded. We decided to invite the Hamilton family to join us for Christmas Eve dinner at the Teammates.

We ran up to the Hamilton family. I shouted, "Mr. and Mrs. Hamilton, hold on!!"

"Mr. and Mrs. Hamilton," Sammy explained. "We just want you to know that if it wasn't for your sons, Shorty and I would never have seen each other again. They really did save our lives."

"Well," Mrs. Hamilton replied. "they shouldn't have worked with that monster in the first place."

"I know," Sammy agreed. "But, as a repayment for helping us, we were wondering if you guys would like to join us for dinner this evening."

Billy and Victor convinced their parents to join in. "Can we, huh? Can we?" They sound like children sometimes, those two.

Their parents accepted, although they would be grounded after this. They were happy to be included. "Yeah! We're going to the Teammates! We're going to the Teammates! We're going to the Teammates!" The boys shouted as they were dancing.

"And, I hate to admit it, Hopkins." Old Man Edward admitted. "But I'm glad you're okay."

Suddenly, a news reporter ran up to them as he yelled, "Billy! Victor! You've JUST won and you are going to the Teammates! What are you going to do now?"

They say what they're going to do: sing and dance all the way there like little kids. The reporter asks if he can come too and the Hamilton Brothers exclaimed together, "Hell yeah!"

As we were all heading towards the Teammates, the Hamilton Brothers and the News Reporter were listening to their favorite song once again and dancing like the silly guys they are.

I whispered to Sammy, "I feel like I'm in a musical right now." She giggled.

****

Later that night at the Teammates, we ran into a lot of familiar faces, a lot of people we knew. We were all at the table chatting with each other. Butchie, Stephanie, and I were talking about the movies while everyone else was focused on the excitement with Shark. Mom was very proud of us for our heroism and everyone was very impressed. Ace, Gloria, Ernie, and even Old Man Edward were all glad Sammy and I were okay.

My Uncle Kevin, my mother's brother, showed up for the party and when he saw me, he shouted, "There's the little hero." He hugged me tightly.

"H...Hi, Uncle Kevin." I said in a funny voice as I was getting crushed.

"And this must be the famous, Sammy," Kevin said as he and Sammy shook hands. "It's a pleasure to meet you."

"Same to you," Sammy replied.

"Hi, Kevin." Butchie chimed in as Stephanie waved.

"Hey there you two lovebirds!" Kevin said as he shook their hands.

Mom rolled her eyes and whispered to Sammy, "I don't even know what to do with that guy."

Suddenly, the door opened. It was my big sister Molly with her boyfriend, Eric. The coincidence is that they have the name as my late grandparents. Funny, huh? She got back from her long trip to Austria, where she went after she graduated from Syracuse University. Molly is quite an adventurer. Sometimes it's like she never wanted to go home.

We were happy to see each other as she sang, "SHORTY HOPKINS! MY BABY BROTHER!!!" Sometimes I feel like I'm in an opera.

She heard about the incident on the car radio and was really impressed. I thanked her.

As Sammy came over to me, I introduced her to Molly. "Molly, this is my good friend, Sammy Johnson. Sammy, this is my big sister, Molly." They shook hands.

Sammy asked me to talk to her privately.

I responded, "Sure, Sammy."

As I got up and walked with her, I looked back at the table. Butchie winked and Stephanie gave me two thumbs up. I smiled and turned back.

My mom came to me and warned me, "Don't overthink this one."

The Hamilton Brothers also saw us in a sweet moment. They still fought like children, arguing who's the hero.

Their mother glared at them to "cool it" as they said together, "Sorry, Ma!"

Billy secretly pinged Victor's ear with his pointer finger. He whistled acting like he didn't do anything wrong as Victor growled at him.

****

When we got outside, it started snowing. We were really thrilled about it. It felt magical, as though the weather was giving us a gift. I also discovered we were under a mistletoe.

I kept looking at the sky as Sammy was staring at me happily. I turned to her and asked, "What?"

Sammy called me her hero because she had been going through a difficult time and I helped her deal with it.

I responded, "Sammy, I think you're the most spectacularly wonderful person I can ever talk to. You really changed my life. I really appreciate that you help me try new things and I'm very grateful to you for helping me manage my emotions better. So thank you."

She tearfully smiled and giggled, "It's my pleasure, Shorty. I'm glad I could help. Your father would be proud of the way you have grown up."

To show my appreciation, I gave Sammy a Christmas card I made. She opened the card, written in my handwriting. "Merry Christmas, Sammy."

"Dear Sammy,

Before you came along, my life was complicated and I didn't even know what to do. Besides, I have no one else like you to help me. You're like my own fairy godmother. When I realized that you lost your parents and Shark abused you, I felt so sorry for you. Your mother and father would be proud of the way you turned out to be. I'm glad I rescued you with a little help from my friends. You really helped me understand things better and you explain real-life so well. I always think you're a perfect guardian angel and teacher to me and everybody around you. You're one of the nicest human beings in the entire universe. You're my everything. I love you so much, Sammy.

Love,

Shorty Hopkins"

As this card touched Sammy's heart, she softly and tearfully said, "Come here." As we leaned forward slowly, we shared our first real kiss under the mistletoe. It was heartfelt and passionate. I felt like I was in a love story. While Sammy and I were kissing, Victor was chasing Billy out the Teammates door. We were both oblivious to what was going on with those fools.

****

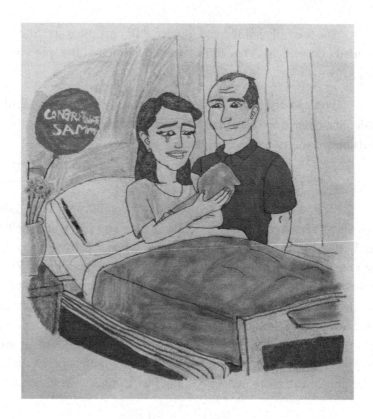

Epilogue

Well this has been a happy ending for all of us. Shark is gone. Victor and Billy both got new jobs at the Teammates and they have nice new girlfriends despite their criminal records.

Victor's girlfriend's name is Diana. She is a huge Michael Jackson fan and does the moonwalk. Billy's girlfriend is Brenda. She came out as a transgender person and Billy couldn't be more accepting of it. Victor and Billy are still childish buffoons.

Butchie and Stephanie now own a successful car-repair company at the Jersey shore. We visit them every summer.

Maureen and Caitlin got married and became the first gay couple in Queens to give birth to healthy quadruplets.

Angie and Dreggs live on a small uncharted island. No one has heard from them since they left the dock aboard their yacht. Did they crash?

My mother and Diane moved to Goshen and now live a happy quiet life. They also met some nice people who are building a new white house with green shutters.

Finally, Sammy and I are still together, living in New York City. We eventually got married and had a child named Timmy. Sammy sometimes reads the Bible to him while I read fairy tales to him. When Timmy gets scared, Sammy says she's going to read *Proverbs 6:20-22:* to him.

"20 My son, observe the commandment of your father And do not forsake the teaching of your mother; 21 Bind them continually on your heart; Tie them around your neck. 22 When you walk about, they will guide you; When you sleep, they will watch over you; And when you awake, they will talk to you"

Thank God Sammy is not overly zealous about religion the way Shark was. Sammy explained that after we defeated Shark, she secretly got his Bible and decided to read heartfelt sentences rather than disturbing ones like Shark did. After Sammy graduated, she and I eventually quit our old jobs. We both work at the Teammates as one of their cover bands. We have been playing live music ever since the fantabulous performance we did during that Christmas party. Sammy is a singer and I became a guitarist. In case you guys thought Sammy wanted to be a therapist, I'll explain. As you know, she quit being my comm. hab. worker to train to be a therapist. After the whole situation with Shark and we became boyfriend and girlfriend, we decided to help disabled people in our own way by writing heartfelt songs. We became successful by using our songs to help disabled people with love and compassion, and like what they say at the end of fairy tales, we lived happily ever after.

The End

In Loving Memory of John J. Glatthaar

Beloved Brother, Cousin, Godfather, Son and Uncle

A Good Man with Strawberries in Banana Cakes and my Big Fan

Tuesday, June 23, 1952-Saturday, June 1, 2013

The oldest of five children, John was born in the Bronx in the Bronx on June 23, 1952 to Joesph B. And Kathleen O'Sullivan Glatthaar. John was raised on Long Island until 1964, when his family moved to White Plains. He resided there ever since. John graduated from Iona Preparatory School and Fordham University (Class of 1975), and worked as a self-employed title examiner in White Plains. His greatest passions were baseball (he loved to talk about the finer points of the game), classic movies, music ('60's and 70's much preferred) and his family. John J. Glatthaar passed away on June 1, 2013, surrounded by his family. John is survived by his parents of White Plains, his brother James of White Plains, Joseph of Chapel Hill, N.C., Thomas of Purchase, and Michael of New York, his sisters-in-law Rose Sharon, Patricia and Jacqueline, his beloved nieces and nephew: Danielle Ha, Kathleen Glatthaar, Thomas Glatthaar and Michele Glatthaar. He was enormously proud of each of them, and fully enjoyed all of their accomplishments. John had a remarkable number of friends, and the Glatthaar family would like to thank all of them for the tremendous outpouring of love and support the past few months.

In Loving Memory of Joseph "Pea Bo" Glatthaar

Beloved Brother, Cousin, Grandfather, Great-Grandfather, and Father

He was also an ultimate true American Hero.

Monday, November 26, 1923-Sunday, December 17, 2017

Joseph B. Glatthaar of White Plains died on December 17, 2017. He was born on November 26, 1923 in Queens, N.Y. To Joseph J. Margaret (Dunn) Glatthaar. He graduated from Jamaica High School and enlisted in the United States Marine Corps in the months after the Pearl Harbor attack. Joseph served in the Pacific as a sergeant with honor and distinction, returning to the States in 1946.

Joseph married Kathleen Mary O'Sullivan on April 28, 1951, and she survives him. He is also survived by his sons James of White Plains, Joseph T. of Chapel Hill, N. C., Thomas of Purchase, and Michael of Atlanta; daughters-in-law Sharon, Patricia and Jacqueline; grandchildren Danielle (Vimy), Kathleen, Thomas H. and Michele; great grandchildren AnneMarie and Lucas; his brother James of New Bern, N.C., as well as many nieces and nephews who will all cherish the many wonderful times they had together. He was predeceased by his oldest son, John, by his brother Arthur, and his sisters Margaret and Dorothy.

Joseph went to Fordham University for his undergraduate degree, and then to NYU Law School for his J.D., both at night and while working full-time during the day and maintaining the responsibilities of a family. He was admitted to the Bar in 1956. Joseph worked at Metropolitan Life Insurance Company for 21 years (starting after high school and returning after the war), 21 years at the law firm of McCarthy Fingar in White Plains. He served on the Advisory Boards of Security Title Guaranty Company, First American Title Insurance Company of New York and National Bank of Westchester, and on the Board of Governors of Westchester Hills Golf Club, where he was a member for nearly fifty years until his death.

In addition to the practice of law (which he loved), Joseph loved baseball and football, always rooting for the New York teams. He loved fishing, both fresh-water and salt-water which he enjoyed well into his 80's. He was never happier than he was spending time with his grandchildren and great grandchildren, who were a source of amending pride and joy to him.

In Loving Memory of Kathleen "Nina" Glatthaar

Beloved Sister, Grandmother, Great-Grandmother and Mother

I love her a push around a peck aka a bushel and a peck.

Monday, September 17, 1928-Tuesday, February 26, 2019

Kathleen M. Glatthaar of White Plains, died on February 26, 2019. Kathleen was born on September 17, 1928 in Bronx, N.Y. to John and Mary (Commane) O'Sullivan. She was raised in the Bronx (and never really left), and graduated from Cathedral High School.

After high school, she worked at Metropolitan Life Insurance Company where she met her future husband. On April 28, 1951 Kathleen married Joseph B. Glatthaar at St. Anthony's Roman Catholic Church, Bronx, N.Y., and they were married for sixty-six years until his death. She is survived by her, sons James of White Plains, Joseph T. of Chapel Hill, N.C., Thomas of Purchase, and Michael of Atlanta; daughters-in-law Sharon, Patricia, and Jacqueline; grandchildren Danielle (Vimy), Kathleen, Thomas H. and Michele; great grandchildren AnneMarie and Lucas, as well as many nieces and nephews, cousins and other relatives, both in the U.S. and in Ireland, all of whom will cherish the many wonderful memories. In addition to Joseph, she was predeceased by her oldest son, John, and by her brothers William and John.

After their wedding Kathleen and Joseph settled in the Bronx. While there they had three of their sons, and added two more sons after moving to Plainview, N.Y. in 1957. The family moved to White Plains in 1964 and have been there since. Kathleen spent her days running the household and raising those five boys, as well as volunteering at St. Bernard's School. It was a full-time job. After her sons were raised she travelled extensively, visiting, among other places, Germany, Russia, Australia, New Zealand, and (every chance she got) Ireland.

Kathleen was a member of Our Lady of Sorrows Church, a long-time member of the Women's Guild at Our Lady of Sorrows, and was, with Joseph, a long-time member of Westchester Hills Golf Club, and she enjoyed nothing more than hosting lunches and dinners there with her extended family. She loved all things and all people from the Bronx and from Ireland. She was also a wonderful and loving grandmother and great grandmother to Danielle, Katie, Tommy, Michele, AnneMarie and Lucas, all of whom affectionately called her "Nina." She was never happier than she was spending time with them. They were, more than anything, a source of unending pride and joy to her.

The family would like to thank Mary Creaven and her team of caregivers, who helped make Kathleen's final few years comfortable, allowing her to live home until the end.